"You feel it too, don't you?" James said, his voice husky.

A small, wry smile twisted Dempsey's lips. "You mean the feeling that we've just been left hanging in space?"

He nodded. "As though there's something unfinished between us."

"As if our brains are saying, 'So where do we go from here?'" she murmured, moistening her lips nervously. "I guess the smart thing would be to say 'It's been interesting, but it's over,' then get on with our lives."

He reached up to touch her face, his thumb caressing her cheek. "Do you always do the smart thing, Dempsey?"

She couldn't keep her mind on what he was saying. He was so close now, she could feel his breath on her lips, see the fine wrinkles around his eyes. She felt the hair on the back of her neck stand up and she inhaled roughly. "Almost never," she admitted in a reluctant whisper, her eyes meeting his.

"Thank goodness." His words were almost a groan as he brought his lips to hers. It felt as though she had been waiting for this kiss forever. . . .

WHAT ARE *LOVESWEPT* ROMANCES?

They are stories of true romance and touching emotion. We believe those two very important ingredients are constants in our highly sensual and very believable stories in the *LOVESWEPT* line. Our goal is to give you, the reader, stories of consistently high quality that may sometimes make you laugh, sometimes make you cry, but are always fresh and creative and contain many delightful surprises within their pages.

Most romance fans read an enormous number of books. Those they truly love, they keep. Others may be traded with friends and soon forgotten. We hope that each *LOVESWEPT* romance will be a treasure—a "keeper." We will always try to publish

LOVE STORIES YOU'LL NEVER FORGET
BY AUTHORS YOU'LL ALWAYS REMEMBER

The Editors

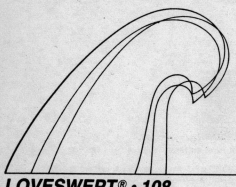

LOVESWEPT® • 108

Billie Green
A Tough Act to Follow

BANTAM BOOKS
TORONTO • NEW YORK • LONDON • SYDNEY • AUCKLAND

A TOUGH ACT TO FOLLOW

A Bantam Book / September 1985

*LOVESWEPT® and the wave device are registered
trademarks of Bantam Books, Inc. Registered in U.S. Patent
and Trademark Office and elsewhere.*

ISBN 0-553-21716-X

Published simultaneously in the United States and Canada

---

*Bantam Books are published by Bantam Books, Inc. Its
trademark, consisting of the words "Bantam Books" and
the portrayal of a rooster, is Registered in U.S. Patent and
Trademark Office and in other countries. Marca Registrada.
Bantam Books, Inc., 666 Fifth Avenue, New York, New
York 10103.*

PRINTED IN THE UNITED STATES OF AMERICA

O   0 9 8 7 6 5 4 3 2 1

To Ginger—beautiful, sensitive laughmaker

One

"Uncle Jamie."

James lowered his book and placed it on the chair-side table. Two small hands framed his face. Hiding his smile, he glanced down at the petite beauty standing in front of him.

"Lovely Uncle Jamie." The blond five-year-old looked up at him with mournful brown eyes as she gently stroked his face. "Don't you think having three brothers is the horriblest thing in the world?"

He gave a soft laugh and pulled his niece's thin pink-leotard-clad body into his lap. "Oh, I don't know, Andy. I think maybe a beautiful ballerina looks even more beautiful when she's surrounded by three hooligans."

Giggling, she leaned her head against his harshly sculptured face and James smiled, inhaling the baby-shampoo smell of her hair. As he held her, he became aware of the slight pang of envy that was nagging at him more and more of late.

Glancing around the den of his sister's house, he was poignantly aware that this was a cozy room in a real home while his own apartment was a mere place to sleep. The difference was right here in his lap and in the sound of the boys squabbling in the backyard. Irene's children never failed to remind him of the silence of his own home.

Frowning suddenly, he wondered exactly when that silence had begun to bother him. Wasn't he satisfied with his life last month? Last week? How many times had he cheerfully agreed with Uncle Charlie and Irene when they told him that his work was his wife and the company's special projects his children?

"Uncle Jamie."

A gruff voice interrupted James's uncomfortable introspection and he glanced up to find seven-year-old Tim staring at him with the strange, soulful expression that sat so often on his young face. "Mikie is eating the dirt in Mom's plants again," he said slowly, world-weary resignation sounding in his voice that bore resemblance to that of a small frog.

"Oh, Lord." James moaned, placing Andrea on the floor before rising and walking toward the patio door.

His oldest nephew, Johnny, followed close behind, tossing a baseball into the air as he walked. "I told him you wouldn't like it, Uncle Jamie, but he just grinned." He rolled his eyes expressively. "You know how Mikie is."

In the backyard James found the culprit sitting beside a large clay pot. With one hand the irrepressible toddler was smearing dirt on his eighteen-month-old face; with the other hand he was swishing the loose black soil in the pot.

James stooped, calmly separating boy from begonia, and carried him into the house. When a reasonable amount of the dirt had been removed from around the protesting mouth, James brought Mikie into the den to join the others.

He stood staring at the four children for a moment until he was sure he had their full attention. "Now. I want all four of you to stay right here where I can see you until your mother gets back. *Don't move.*" He gave them a ferocious glare that brought only giggles. "And Johnny," he added as he returned to his chair, "you're the oldest; for heaven's sake, watch your baby brother."

Leaning back in the leather rocker, he picked up his book. After he found himself reading the same page for the third time, he put aside the spy thriller. His mind was suddenly too much taken up with his future. Were Irene and the old man right? Was James letting real life slip by him? Had he gotten so caught up in his work that he was using it as a substitute for a normal life?

He couldn't even remember how he had gotten to this point. Somewhere along the way it had simply happened. Somehow the time had never been right for personal involvement. There had always been women, but never that one special woman.

Shifting restlessly, he raised his eyes to the ceiling, annoyed at the direction his thoughts were taking. James had never tried to avoid facts, and the fact was he had always been too busy to let a relationship develop. Too involved in his work, too absorbed with his steady progression within the company to allow much room for anything else. But in his defense, James knew he had never found anything in his personal life to match the excitement of working through an intricate deal that he alone could bring to fruition.

He turned his head to gaze unseeingly out the window, the sound of young voices providing background music for his moody introspection.

Why was he suddenly questioning the way he lived? he wondered in irritation. He liked his life the way it was. If he didn't, he would change it. Anyway, he thought, a slight frown shaping his strong lips, who in hell said he couldn't have his work *and* a family? It wasn't too late. Thirty-six was the prime of life. He had plenty of time to acquire his own miniature ballerina, his own pint-sized rogue.

"Tim," he said absently, his eyes on the children but his mind still dwelling on the unaccountable twist his thoughts had taken. "Stop putting that stuff in Andy's hair. Andy, it wasn't necessary to punch Tim."

He rubbed the bridge of his nose in an unconscious gesture. Any thought of marriage naturally lead him to Chloe—tall, lovely, *ready* Chloe. Ready for marriage, ready for children. She would make a dedicated mother, a loyal wife. Maybe it was time he did something about Chloe. He could have it all. So what if it wouldn't be what Irene and Steve had? James didn't have such great expectations. Marriage with Chloe would be stable and comfortable. That was enough. Surely it was enough.

Irene would be pleased at his change of heart, he thought with a wry smile. How many times had she told him that he borrowed her family because he didn't want to take the time to start his own? James knew that his sister didn't resent his fondness for her children, but Irene was a fixer, an arranger. She wanted everyone to be as fulfilled as she was. At least if he married Chloe, his sister would no longer be able to nag him about his dedication to his job.

The thought of his work brought a vision of a smiling round face and twinkling blue eyes. Damn Uncle Charlie. Damn that wonderful old codger. As if the normal pressures of his job weren't enough, Uncle Charlie had to add a new problem. What a curve ball he'd thrown, and something was going to have to be done about it . . . and him! James had never stopped to consider his maternal uncle's age, but age was obviously getting to him. Why else would he be trying to wreak havoc with James's life? This last stunt was too much. It couldn't be written off as another of Uncle Charlie's little practical jokes. His uncle was definitely getting out of hand.

He exhaled roughly. Somehow he had to undo the damage Uncle Charlie had done before anyone found out about it. Didn't that old fool know he would be in real trouble if his little joke were discovered?

His eyes closed in exasperation at the thought. Tonight, after he spoke at the Chamber of Commerce dinner, he would take care of Uncle Charlie's mischief. And then he would take steps to see that it never happened again.

The high-pitched sound of children's voices ceased for a moment as the doorbell rang, then picked up again with increased force as James walked toward the front door.

"Johnny, stop throwing the ball in the house," he called over his shoulder as he swung open the door. "I'm sorry," he said, glancing at the young woman standing on the porch. "The kids are—"

Suddenly his words died away and whatever he had intended to say fled his mind. She was speaking as she smiled up at him, but James couldn't seem to take in what she was saying. He was being attacked by the strangest feeling. He felt exhilarated yet somehow loose, as though he had taken a drug.

As he stood in bemused silence his gaze drifted over the small woman, searching for a clue to help solve the mystery of her strange effect on him. He took in every visible inch of her. Twisted around her forehead was a lavender silk scarf that didn't even begin to tame the dark curls spreading wildly about her shoulders. Slacks in a violent shade of green hugged her hips and thighs and a white lace blouse loosely covered her upper torso, letting just a hint, a suggestion, of tantalizing flesh show through.

It was an attractive, vibrant picture, but there was

nothing there to cause such a strong reaction. He watched her small bow-shaped lips move in speech and became more aware of the new sensation; it was as though something inside him that had been shackled were suddenly breaking free.

Returning his gaze to her face, he felt an uncontrollable smile stretching his lips. It was a unique face, a beautiful face, but not the kind of beauty that brought silent awe. It was the kind that made you feel more alive just to look at it, the kind that made you want to laugh from pure joy.

This was crazy, he told himself. His reaction, so completely out of character, also made him want to laugh. Struggling silently to regain control of his senses, he tried to tune in on what she was saying as he forced himself to deny the strange sensation. Triumphantly, he felt reality take hold once more.

Dempsey sensed that her smile, her ace-salesman smile, was slipping as the man in the doorway continued to stare at her, first with a stunned expression, then amusement, then with a touch of cynicism that added sharp lines to his strong, lean face. She reached up to touch her hair.

"What's wrong?" She grinned as she leaned against the doorjamb, liking the sparks of humor she saw appearing in his brown eyes. The amusement seemed to be turned inward, as though he were laughing at himself. "Do I have a smudge on my nose? A piece of chive on my tooth?"

She had expected the door to be opened by the

usual busy homemaker or even an impatient maid. She had definitely not expected a brown-haired, brown-eyed hunk dressed in evening clothes.

"I told myself that this would be the last doorbell I rang today," she said confidingly as she bent to lift the things that were sitting on the porch beside her. "My feet are killing me. This neighborhood was supposed to be a glory hole. Some glory hole. What is it with people around here? Doesn't anyone believe in free enterprise?"

As she continued her unbroken stream of wry comments, she walked past him into the entry hall, carrying her equipment with her. "You wouldn't believe how many doors I've had slammed in my face today. If I weren't so quick on my feet, I'd have a cauliflower nose by now."

"Vacuum cleaners?" His comment was punctuated by a quiet, attractive chuckle as he glanced down at the machine she was dragging behind her. "You sell vacuum cleaners?"

She opened her gray eyes wide, giving him an incredulous look. "Vacuum cleaners?" she echoed indignantly. "Did you say vacuum cleaners? Let me tell you, sir or madam, this is no mere vacuum cleaner. It happens to be the miracle machine of the eighties. The only thing this modern marvel won't do is slice and dice. It sucks up all the pesky little bits of grit and grime that defeat ordinary machines; it shampoos your carpet to within an inch of its life; and with a few simple attachments, it will style your hair, dry your delicate undies, and even make a passable beef jerky."

"Okay." He held up his hand, his craggy face and dark eyes reflecting his amusement. "I'll take your word for it." He shook his head and added, "Somehow, I'm having a problem connecting you"—he ran his eyes down the length of her—"with door-to-door selling of vacuum cleaners."

"Now you sound like my boss." She grimaced. "He was a little reluctant to hire me. I had to do some pretty fast talking to get the job."

He smiled. "But you've proven him wrong by selling a record number of vacuum cleaners."

"Of course," she said, nodding, then switched in midstream and shook her head in a negative motion. "Actually, I've been on the job for three days and haven't sold a single machine." Her brow wrinkled in bewilderment. "I don't know what I'm doing wrong. Your next-door neighbor, Mrs. Olsen, is typical. She sounded genuinely enthusiastic when she let me in. She watched my demonstration, played all her Jimmy Durante records for me, and fed me zucchini bread while we listened." She sighed. "Then she told me her brother gets all her appliances for her wholesale."

She stared for a moment at those gorgeous laughing eyes. He really was an attractive man. She liked the way he watched her face as she talked, the way he seemed to absorb what she was saying rather than think about what he was going to say next, as some people did.

But she wasn't here to admire the scenery, Dempsey reminded herself. She was here to make a living. If she didn't sell something pretty soon, she would be unemployed again . . . and her landlady wouldn't like that one bit.

Bending down, she began to unwind the cord on the cleaner. "Where can I plug this in?" She looked past him into the den. "I know you're going to love this demonstration. It's the best part of my—"

She broke off and glanced at the man beside her, then nodded toward the den. "Is he allowed to eat the goldfish?"

The man beside her swung around to see the small boy that had caught her attention, one arm in the aquarium up to his elbow, the other trying to stuff a vigorously protesting goldfish into his mouth.

Dempsey followed behind him, carefully taking in the room and its occupants. There weren't actually ten or twelve children in the room as she had first thought, only four, but they were certainly a lively bunch. The little girl hopped on one foot and squealed as the tiny fisherman was deftly relieved of one grateful goldfish. The oldest boy howled with laughter while another somber-looking boy merely groaned and crossed his eyes.

Dempsey's host held the youngest boy an arm's length away from his immaculate dinner jacket and eyed the oldest sternly. "I thought I told you to watch Mikie."

"I did. I watched him eat the goldfish. It was really neat."

Dempsey watched as he shook his head and carried the wet boy from the room. Turning to the remaining children, she winked and smiled, then finished unwinding the vacuum cleaner cord.

"What are you doing?"

She glanced down at the petite blond girl. "I'm going to show you how this works. Would you— what's your name?"

"Andrea."

"Would you like that, Andrea?"

The little girl shrugged doubtfully.

"Well, it may not be interesting for you, but I'm sure your father will be thrilled."

Andrea collapsed on an ottoman in giggles. "He's not our father. He's Uncle Jamie." She turned her head toward her brothers. "She thought Uncle Jamie was Daddy." Her huge brown eyes turned back to Dempsey. "That's Johnny and Tim. Daddy's out of town and Mommy's gone shopping. She's going to buy me a surprise, but not Johnny and Tim because they broke Mr. Thompson's kitchen window with a fly ball that Johnny says was probably a world record except Mom wouldn't let him measure it before Mr. Thompson got it out of the bowl of oatmeal and threw it in the trash." Dempsey was beginning to get dizzy when Andrea finally paused for air and added cheerfully, "Uncle Jamie loves to baby-sit us."

Dempsey nodded solemnly. "He does look as though he's enjoying himself."

"What's your name?" Tim asked, and Dempsey smiled at his husky voice.

"Dempsey Turner-Riley," she said, reaching out to shake his hand. "Salesman par excellence . . . or a reasonable facsimile thereof."

Suddenly Uncle Jamie was standing beside her. "Dempsey." He said the name slowly, as though tasting it. "It suits you. It's unusual and . . . emphatic."

Emphatic? How did he know that? Dempsey gave him a curious smile as he held out his hand. "I'm James Halloran, and I see you've met the brood."

She nodded, her eyes twinkling. "All except Mikie. Is Mikie two?"

"Not quite. Irene keeps telling me it's just a stage, but I have a feeling Mikie is going to be Mikie for the rest of his life."

"Dempsey. *Dempsey*, I can dance." Andrea interrupted them to pirouette across the floor.

"You certainly can," Dempsey said admiringly. "You look like a fairy princess. I took lessons when I was your age, but somehow it's not the same when you're chubby."

James gave her a disbelieving look. "Chubby? There's no way you were ever chubby."

She glanced up at him. "Are you kidding? For years all the kids called me Dempsey Dumpster."

She cocked her head when she heard his laugh again. It was a low sound that seduced rather than startled the listener. He was very close beside her now, and Dempsey should have felt awkward, standing there in the middle of the room, staring up at him, but she didn't. She wasn't at all uncomfortable. Somehow the warm, intense look in his eyes prevented that feeling as an unaccountable intimacy began to grow between them.

"Is Dempsey a family name?"

She nodded slowly, trying to rid herself of the curious light-headed feeling she was experiencing. "It was my uncle's name. Actually, my first name is Eleanor, but I don't use it. No one . . . well, almost no one calls me Eleanor anymore."

"Eleanor Dempsey Turner-Riley. That's quite a mouthful."

She grinned and nodded again. "That's why I use Dempsey Turner-Riley as a stage name. It has a certain ring to it."

His eyebrows drew together in curiosity. "Stage name? Are you an actress?"

"Dempsey." Johnny pulled on her arm to interrupt them. "See my handcuffs."

She glanced down at the shiny metal cuffs the boy held, and whistled in admiration. "Those are handcuffs, all right. They look like real, regulation handcuffs."

"Ha! I fooled you," he said, laughing in delight. "They're not regulation. These are real crook's handcuffs. My Uncle Charlie gave them to me. He's not really my uncle. He's my great-uncle. He's my mom's uncle and Uncle Jamie's uncle."

"Is he a policeman?"

"He's retired, but these are a real live criminal's handcuffs. Uncle Charlie called him Sneaky Pete and the police department was so proud of Uncle Charlie for capturing him that they gave him these handcuffs as a souvenir. Didn't they, Uncle Jamie?"

Before James could reply, Andrea pushed Johnny out of the way and began bouncing up and down in front of them to get Dempsey's attention. "Dempsey, watch this; watch this. Is this the way you used to do it?"

Dempsey watched the little girl do an intricate step, but she simply couldn't concentrate with James standing so close. If he would just move a step away, maybe she could remember what she was supposed to be doing. Maybe the hair on her arms wouldn't stand up as though he emitted an electrical charge.

She absently began to rewind the cord, then suddenly felt his hand covering hers. She looked down at it, then up to his strong, lean face.

"You haven't given us a demonstration yet," he said. His voice had sharpened with the words, but his eyes seemed to convey a meaning different from his words. If it weren't so ridiculous, she would have said she saw yearning in his dark eyes. In the next second the strange look in his eyes disappeared, as though it had never been there. Now they held only amusement . . . and perhaps a touch of self-mockery. She wondered what went on in his mind to cause such a multitude of swiftly passing emotions.

She cleared her throat nervously and opened her mouth to speak, then hesitated when she felt something cold and metallic slide around her wrist.

"See," Johnny said triumphantly. "They really work. There's no way a crook could get out of them."

James and Dempsey looked down at the same time to find their wrists joined by the handcuffs.

"Gee, that's neat, Johnny," Dempsey said. "But I think you'd better unlock them now. I'm going to have to leave soon."

"Without giving us a real look at the miracle machine of the eighties?" James asked.

Staring up at him, she inhaled sharply as she

caught a glimpse of the vulnerable pleading she had seen moments earlier. Somehow it didn't fit, and the incongruity made her uneasy.

"Are you really interested in buying a vacuum cleaner?" she asked.

"I might be." His words were abrupt, as though he were annoyed, then once again his face changed and there was a deliberate sensuality in the look he gave her. "It just depends on who's selling it."

"Uncle Jamie." Johnny stood close to his uncle and gave him a worried look.

"Just a second, Johnny," he said, then to Dempsey, "Stay until my sister gets back . . . please. She might need a vacuum cleaner."

There was nothing studied in the plea, and she was almost sure his words were involuntary. He changed so quickly; it was like being on a carousel that was out of control. She laughed shakily and shook her head. "You don't really believe that."

"It may be exactly what she needs. Then she would be very upset if I let you get away," James said quickly.

As he stared down at her he wondered silently why he was pressing her not to leave. Why did he feel this strange urgency, as though it were of great importance that she stay? It didn't make any kind of sense. He shook his head slightly and his mouth tightened stubbornly. Why did he have to explain everything? Maybe Irene really did need a vacuum cleaner.

"Uncle Jamie." Johnny's voice was more urgent this time.

Reluctantly, James turned his attention away from

Dempsey's big gray eyes to his nephew. "What is it, Johnny?"

"I can't find the key."

"We'll look for it later; it's probably in your toy box," he said absently, then turned his gaze back to Dempsey. "Just wait a few more minutes. I know Irene—" He broke off suddenly and glanced down at Johnny, frowning in consternation. "What key?"

But Johnny didn't have to answer. The expression on his face was answer enough.

After a startled moment, Dempsey began to laugh. She couldn't help it. The expression on James's face was a study in comic dismay as he stared down at the handcuffs that bound them.

"Don't say it," she muttered, raising her eyes to the ceiling. "Don't say it."

James gave her a harried glance. "Don't say what?"

"I'm having to bite my tongue to keep from saying, 'Recently I find myself becoming rather attached to you.' "

He gave a short bark of laughter, then shook his head as he listened to Johnny's anxious explanation. "I gave it to Tim to hold. He said he put it down on the coffee table, but it's not there now."

"Tim?"

"I did, Uncle Jamie," Tim said solemnly. "I put it right here on the coffee table."

"I know where it is."

They all turned to stare at Andrea as she half bounced, half danced across the room, pleased that she had their undivided attention at last.

"I know where it is. I know where it is," she called gaily, jumping up and down.

"Where is it, you half-pint creep?" Johnny demanded threateningly. "What did you do with my key?"

Andrea stopped bouncing and gave him a haughty look as the battle lines were drawn. "I didn't touch your dumb old key. And Mommy told you not to call me a creep anymore."

"Andy, you stupid baby turkey, I'll—"

"That's enough," James said quietly but firmly. He moved toward Andy, then stopped short as he realized he was attached to Dempsey. He grinned suddenly, then turned to his niece. "Andy, do you know where the key is?"

She nodded slowly.

"Where is it, honey?"

"Mikie took it."

"Mikie—" he began, then his eyes widened. "Oh, Lord, *Mikie*!"

Every head in the room turned as one toward the chubby, smiling boy who was in the process of shoving something small and metallic into his mouth.

Two

Chaos erupted as James moved quickly toward the boy, dragging a startled Dempsey behind. He was brought up short when she tripped over Tim, who gave a series of gruff yelps, adding to the general confusion. When they finally reached Mikie, the boy's hands were resting in his lap and an angelic smile curved his baby mouth.

"Mikie," James said anxiously. "Open your mouth, fella."

Mikie looked up at the crowd around him and obediently opened his mouth, sticking out his pink tongue until it touched his chin. This was obviously a routine Mikie was used to, but a quick examination showed no sign of the key.

James ran a hand through his hair and gave a harried look around the room as though seeking help. "Now, what in hell am I—"

He broke off and Dempsey saw a mixture of relief and wariness grow in his eyes as a tall, slender blond woman walked into the den. It didn't take much deduction to know that this was James's sister. She was an older version of Andrea.

"What's up?" Irene asked, eyeing Dempsey curiously as she held out her hand. "Hi, I'm Irene Calder."

When no one spoke, Irene glanced at James, then back to Dempsey. "I'm late I know, but I had to wait forever for those drapes." She paused, glancing around her in curiosity. "James, aren't you going to introduce us?"

"Irene," he began hesitantly. "Stay calm. There's nothing to get excited about."

"Am I excited?" she asked with a laugh. "I think I can meet someone new without panicking."

"Irene, Mikie—"

"Mikie?" she asked, glancing down at her youngest son, then creases of alarm appeared between her brows. "What's wrong with Mikie?" she asked anxiously as she stooped down to pick him up. "He didn't drink the fabric softener again, did he?"

"No, Mom." Johnny's eyes were shining with excitement. "It wasn't fabric softener this time. It was—"

"We think maybe he swallowed a key," James interrupted, trying desperately to appear calm.

"A key! Oh, dear heaven!" She moaned, sitting down with an unconcerned Mikie in her arms. "What are we going to do? Sweet heaven, a key! What if they have to operate? James, they can't operate while Steve's out of town! What—"

Suddenly everyone was talking at once. Irene was rocking back and forth, talking to Mikie, to her absent husband, and to her brother in turn. James was running his fingers through his already rumpled hair as he tried to answer questions and think of a solution at the same time. The three oldest children were quickly drawn into the hysteria, their voices growing louder and louder.

Placing two fingers between her lips, Dempsey let out a piercing whistle. Everyone turned to look at her, and the room fell abruptly silent. "Why don't we call your doctor and ask what to do?"

"Yes. Yes, of course," Irene said in relief. "That's what Steve would do if he were here—and why in hell isn't he here?" she added, shaking her head in exasperation.

James gave Dempsey a grateful smile as Irene carried Mikie on her hip to the telephone in the hall. "Thanks," he said. "You saved my life."

She smiled and shrugged. "It's all part of the service. I also slay dragons and unclog sinks." She felt his hand clasp hers and suddenly the hairs on her arm went crazy again as his thumb began to move slowly back and forth over the palm of her hand.

"I'll remember that the next time I run into a dragon."

As she stared up at him her mouth went strangely dry, and she couldn't have spoken if her life had depended on it. There was an intensity in the way he looked at her that was drawing her toward him, an intensity that grew with each passing second. She couldn't seem to dredge up enough willpower to break away from his gaze.

Why was this happening to her? He was a total stranger, a very complex stranger, and she knew she was way out of her depth. Yet she felt in some way tied to him, as though something deeper than her consciousness recognized him. Maybe *cuffed*—not tied—to him would have been a better way to put it, she thought ruefully. It took outside interference to return Dempsey to reality, and she turned gratefully to Irene as the woman returned to the den with Mikie.

"Dr. Martin said Mikie will have to be X-rayed," Irene said. There was no panic in her voice now. It was as though she had pulled up strength because strength was needed. "He said not to worry; Mikie will be fine. He just wants to make sure the key didn't lodge in the trachea or the pulmonary lung fills."

As she talked, Irene pulled on Mikie's socks and shoes. "He said to bring him to the clinic and get it over with now."

"We'll take the station wagon and—" She stopped abruptly, staring at James and Dempsey. "Why are you handcuffed together?"

"Which key do you think Mikie swallowed?" James asked, his words colored with resigned amusement.

Irene's lips began to twitch. She put her hand over her mouth, but within seconds the room was filled with the sound of their combined laughter, laughter that held a great deal of relief.

Five minutes later they were all in Irene's station wagon headed for the clinic. Irene drove and Mikie sat happily beside her in his safety seat. James and Dempsey, of necessity, occupied the second seat, and in the third, facing the back of the car, were the three remaining children.

As James and Irene talked, Dempsey looked out the window, thinking how intimate she had become with this family in such a short time, not only physically because of the handcuffs but also emotionally. She came in as a stranger and within minutes she had felt a part of the boisterous group.

Suddenly she stiffened as she felt James's hand on her thigh. She glanced at him, but he was still speaking quietly to Irene, his eyes on the back of his sister's head. His fingers clasped hers and the back of his hand began sliding up and down the smooth fabric of the slacks, not merely caressing but endeavoring to learn the muscles and flesh.

She should slap him, she thought as electric waves shot through her body. She would, she told herself. She would slap him . . . in just a moment.

James stopped listening to Irene, losing his train of thought as he felt the warmth of Dempsey's leg beneath his fingers. He couldn't understand how his hand came to be on her thigh. It wasn't like him to make crude advances. But now that it was there, he couldn't bring himself to remove it. It was as though the feel of her was mesmerizing him just as the sight of her had earlier.

"Does Dempsey have growing pains too, Uncle Jamie?"

James turned his head and found himself nose to nose with Tim, whose solemn eyes were trained earnestly on James's face.

"Mom rubs my leg when I have growing pains," he said gruffly. "Is that why you're rubbing Dempsey's leg?"

James frowned. "How many times have you been told to keep your seat belt buckled?" he asked, hedging his nephew's question.

As quickly as Tim resumed his seat, Johnny took his place, leaning over the seat to see if his uncle really was rubbing Dempsey's leg. Even though James's and Dempsey's hands were now lying innocently between them on the seat, he gave his uncle a suspicious glance.

After a moment of silence when he felt the back of his neck grow annoyingly red, James said grimly, "Johnny, do you know what happens to little boys who get too curious?"

"No, sir," Johnny said, eyeing his uncle's stern features.

"They get throttled until their cute little faces turn black and their adorable little ears fall off."

Johnny gave a snort of surprised laughter, then collapsed in his seat. The car was filled with the sound of the three children's giggles.

"James," Irene said in irritation. "I wish you would stop encouraging them. Quiet down, you three."

"Encouraging them?" he muttered in exasperation.

He couldn't see Dempsey laughing and he couldn't hear her laughing, but he was almost sure she was laughing. Not at the children, at him. When she turned toward him and whispered, "It serves you right, 'Uncle Jamie,' " he was positive.

Dempsey smiled when James turned to stare moodily out the window. She was glad he was too annoyed to wonder why she hadn't removed his hand from her leg. It was something she didn't care to examine too closely . . . and she definitely didn't want him wondering about it.

At the clinic, James's mood switched once again as they tried to keep track of the older children while Mikie was being X-rayed. It wasn't an easy task. As though someone had pushed a hidden button, all three of them became superactive. She was so busy trying to keep track of them, Dempsey didn't have time to notice the peculiar looks their joined hands were receiving from the others in the room.

When Irene returned to the waiting room, Dempsey was straining to get Andy out from under a pregnant woman's chair while James caught hold of Johnny and Tim by their respective collars. All motion ceased at the sight of Irene and the doctor with the grinning boy between them.

"Dr. Martin said it wasn't pressing against anything vital," she said with a smile of relief. "Now all we have to do is wait for the key to show up."

Dr. Martin smiled at them, then suddenly his eyes rested on James's and Dempsey's joined hands. "The missing key?" he asked, indicating the cuffs with a nod.

"I'm afraid so," James verified ruefully.

It was obvious that the trim and tanned doctor was having difficulty keeping a straight face. "I would say you need the police department. There's a precinct station down the street. They should have a master key."

"That was a waste of time," James said, his voice totally disgusted.

The three adults were now seated on the comfortable overstuffed sofa in Irene's den after a fruitless trip to the police station.

"Oh, I don't know," Dempsey said. "It wasn't a total loss. That sergeant makes a heck of a cup of tea."

James shot her a grim look. "I'm glad you enjoyed yourself." He frowned. "I didn't know there were that many keys in the world. I would think one of them would have fit."

Dempsey shrugged. "I guess Sneaky Pete was sneakier than we gave him credit for. He wanted to make sure the police couldn't unlock these cuffs." She reached down and rubbed her wrist where a faint red mark showed.

"I'm so sorry," Irene said, shaking her head as she grimaced at Dempsey. "You seem to have been dragged into the midst of our usual uproar."

Dempsey grinned at the attractive woman sitting beside her. "I like it." She paused, glancing at James, then back to Irene. "I don't think we were ever introduced. I'm Dempsey Turner-Riley . . . and I think your family is even more interesting than Mrs. Olsen's Jimmy Durante records."

Irene gave her a quizzical look. "How did you meet Mrs. Olsen?"

"I was trying to sell her a vacuum cleaner," Dempsey explained, indicating her equipment with the wave of her free hand.

"She gets all her stuff from her brother wholesale." James, Irene, and Dempsey all spoke at the same time, then laughed.

Dempsey shrugged philosophically. "At least I managed to get the recipe for her zucchini bread."

"She's proud of her baking," Irene said. "I'm glad you humored her and stayed awhile. Since her husband's death she has too much time on her hands."

"Why don't you ask her to baby-sit?" James asked dryly, then glanced at the grandfather clock on the opposite wall. "Oh, hell! Look at the time. With all that's happened I forgot all about the Chamber of Commerce dinner. I have to be there in twenty-five minutes." He stood up, then looked down as Dempsey's hand followed him.

"Damn!"

"Oh, James." Irene's lips began to twitch again, but her voice was sympathetic. "And you're the main speaker. What are you going to do?" She paused thoughtfully. "What about a locksmith?"

"Do you know how long it would take to get a locksmith out here?" James asked, shaking his head. "A hacksaw might do it. Does Steve have one?"

"You're kidding. You know Steve's no good with his hands. We have one hammer with a broken handle and a set of screwdrivers some misguided fool gave him for Christmas." She paused. "I could check with the neighbors . . . or maybe we could buy one."

"There's no time for that." He rubbed the bridge of

his nose, his eyes growing thoughtful. "We'll have to think of something else."

Dempsey leaned her head back as they talked. The close relationship between these two was obvious. She didn't know a brother and sister could also be friends. It felt comfortable being around them, as though a little of this . . . this warm family feeling were rubbing off on her. She wondered with a small frown what her life would have been like if she hadn't been an only child. Maybe if she hadn't, things would have been different. Maybe . . .

Suddenly Dempsey was brought back to the present by the silence around her. James was staring at her, his eyes narrowed in speculation. "Are you thinking what I'm thinking?" He was speaking to Irene, but his eyes never left Dempsey.

Dempsey turned to the woman beside her and found her staring too. "It's crazy, but it might work," Irene said slowly.

"What about clothes?" James asked.

Dempsey looked from one to the other. Why were they staring at her like that? Had she missed something?

"I think I have something that will work." Excitement grew in her eyes as she spoke.

"What are you talking about?" Dempsey asked in confusion.

"Come on," James said, pulling her to her feet. Irene followed them, carrying Mikie, as James led Dempsey into the hall, then through a door into a large bedroom.

"Wait a minute," Dempsey protested as Irene sat

Mikie on the bed and began riffling through the clothes that hung in a walk-in closet. "What's going on?"

"This will do," Irene said, pulling a red strapless dress from the closet. "You see, she can wear the lace blouse over it as a jacket."

James nodded and without a word pushed Dempsey back on the bed. She bounced twice, then looked up to see Mikie's face hovering over her. He smiled a charming baby smile and his pudgy hands came down to pat her face, then Dempsey received her first upside-down, slightly damp kiss.

When she felt hands at her waist, she looked away from Mikie to find Irene pulling the lace blouse out of her waistband and James unhooking the green slacks. Dempsey was beginning to get annoyed at the way they talked to each other as though she were invisible. At least she had finally figured out what was going on. It was clear now that Irene and James were preparing her to go to the Chamber of Commerce dinner.

Reaching down, Dempsey grabbed at the various hands at her waist. They both glanced up and stared at her, Irene expectantly, James impatiently. She smiled sweetly at the two people bent over her. "Don't you think one of you should at least ask me if I'll go to the dinner?"

James raised one sharply defined eyebrow and glanced down at the handcuffs that joined them. "I can't see that you have much of a choice."

"*James,*" Irene scolded. "Dempsey's right. We haven't even asked her."

He smiled slowly and the sensuality of his full lower lip became even more apparent. Once again Dempsey became caught up in the strange look in his eyes and Irene and Mikie were forgotten completely as he spoke. "Dempsey Turner-Riley, would you give me the pleasure of your company at the Chamber of Commerce dinner?"

She inhaled slowly to steady her erratic pulse, then tipped her head as though considering the question. "Yes, thank you, Mr. Halloran," she said after a moment. "I believe I will."

"Good," he said briskly, and she wondered if she had imagined the slow flame in his dark eyes. "Now, let's get her slacks off."

As Irene worked on the buttons of her blouse, James slid the zipper down and began to pull at the slacks. After a moment Dempsey said slowly, "You know, I hate to be picky, but do you think you could let Irene do that while you turn your head?"

He stared for a moment at the creamy flesh of her stomach above the bright purple bikini panties, then grinned and turned away.

Irene didn't even pause in her work, but moved to help Dempsey slide out of the slacks, then finished the buttons on the lace blouse. "It's a good thing you're not wearing a bra, Dempsey," she said. "We might have had to cut it."

Suddenly Dempsey's skin began to tingle and she felt James's large thumb making circles on her palm again. She glanced up and met his eyes in the mirror on the opposite wall. Clutching at the edges of the blouse, she said calmly, "Close your eyes or you'll have to drag me kicking and screaming to that dinner."

Irene glanced up and frowned. "James, this is no time to get cute."

James laughed, but after a wicked wink at the mirror, closed his eyes obediently. When Irene turned back to Dempsey there was a surprised, speculative look in her eyes. After a moment she shrugged and began to help Dempsey step into the red dress.

In a surprisingly short time Dempsey was clad in red dress, lace overblouse, sheer panty hose, and gold evening sandals that were only a hair too large.

"There," Irene said. "Now all we have to do is run a comb through your hair and add a little lipstick and we're done." She reached up to remove the braided band from Dempsey's hair.

Turning away from the mirror, James surveyed Irene's handiwork. After a moment he frowned. Dempsey stood beside him with her shoulders hunched, her arms crossed beneath her breasts. "Stand up straight," he said, giving her a questioning look.

"You sound like my mother," she muttered, then threw him a stubborn look. "If I stand up straight, this dress will be around my waist."

There was that smile again, that sizzling sensuality that told her he didn't find the idea repulsive.

"Oh," Irene said, glancing down at her own generous bosom. "I didn't think of that. Here, let me get some pins." She hastily pinned the back of the dress, then stood back and both she and James looked Dempsey over carefully.

"Perfect," Irene said in satisfaction.

"Perfect," James echoed softly.

As they walked out of the bedroom, Irene draped a silk scarf over their hands to conceal the unconventional bracelets, then she and the children followed James and Dempsey through the kitchen and waved as the couple stepped into the garage.

There were two cars in the garage and James moved toward a gleaming white Porsche, then stopped suddenly. He looked down at their hands, then at the car, then back to their hands.

"My left hand," he muttered incomprehensibly, then slowly, grimly, he said, "No one drives my car except me." He raised his eyes to hers and repeated the words with a great deal of visible pain. "No one drives my car except me."

"I'm sorry," Dempsey said, giving him a sympathetic smile. "But I either drive or run alongside the car."

"There's got to be another way." He was thoughtfully silent for a moment. "Here. Try this." He moved her to his side, drawing his left hand under his right arm. "Now crawl over the gear shift to the passenger seat."

The next five minutes were straight out of a Three Stooges movie. At one point her knee was resting against his eye. Her laughter and his grunts of pain and muttered curses made an interesting combination of sounds.

"Are you all right out there?" Irene called from the doorway as they finally managed to arrange themselves in the correct seats.

"We're fine," James said roughly, his breath coming in short gasps.

Dempsey had to smother the laughter that threatened to overcome her when she saw the way his hair stood up in spiky tufts. Swallowing heavily, she said, "Now let me see you shift the gears."

He raised his left hand—and consequently her right—and found the knob of the floor shift. "Damn," he breathed after a few seconds. "My left hand can't be that weak."

"It's because you're going at it sideways. You couldn't possibly apply enough pressure without getting a hernia." She could tell by his piercing look that he didn't appreciate her logic. She shrugged. "I could shift for you, but I'm afraid we'd end up stripping the gears."

Silence filled the car for long seconds, then he said tightly, "All right. All right. You can drive it."

"Can I honestly, Mr. Halloran?" she said with eyes widened in awe. "Gee, sir, I never expected anything like this. Wait until I tell the gang."

"Are you through?"

She bit her lip. "Yes, sir."

"Good. Then let's change places." He began to move to the right, pulling her to the left. "Lift up a little, for heaven's sake, so I can move under you." They moved again and suddenly she was in his lap. "Dempsey," he said with deadly calm.

"Yes, James?"

"Do you know where I'm sitting?"

"On the gearshift?"

"That's right, and I'm not into that kind of thing.

Now"—he lifted her up—"*move over.*" He had one hand on her stomach and the other on her breast as he lifted and pushed, but Dempsey decided it was not the time to worry about her modesty.

At last she sat in the driver's seat, her head resting on the steering wheel. Their combined breathing sounded loud and harsh in the small car. Raising her head, she glanced at James. "Wouldn't it have been easier if we had simply gotten out of the car?"

"Maybe," he said, and suddenly she saw a gleam of amusement in his eyes that surprised her. "But it wouldn't have been nearly as much fun."

She felt the heat rise in her cheeks as she realized he had been as aware as she of where his hands had held her. Before she could pull up a smart comment he was urging her to back out of the garage so that they could be on their way.

"Turn the wheel to the left. No, more . . . more— son of a— Do you see the station wagon?"

She simply ignored him, even when his instructions became louder, even when the grinding of gears brought a sound from him that was a cross between a groan and a prayer, and continued to back out of the garage.

When she reached the street at last she chanced a glance in his direction. "I was a good foot away from that garbage can," she said righteously.

"An inch," he said hoarsely. "No, a centimeter. I could *feel* the trash in that can." He paused, exhaling slowly. "Just keep your eyes on the—oh, hell!"

He closed his eyes weakly as Dempsey swerved to miss a U-Haul truck that appeared out of nowhere and didn't open them again until they reached the hotel. When she pulled under the canopied drive, Dempsey could feel his muscles relaxing as though he were forcing each one to unfreeze.

"We're here," she said brightly as the door was opened for her by a young man in top hat and tails.

The look James gave her was not pretty, and at any other time Dempsey might have feared for her life, but at that moment she was wondering if she or James was going to crawl over the gearshift console.

She shouldn't have wondered. Within seconds he had his door open and was hauling her across, oblivious to the curious stares of the doorman. Inside the hotel, he hurried her across the lobby.

"Wait," she whispered urgently. When he stopped, she reached up with one hand to smooth his hair and straighten his satin bow tie. James stared down at her for a moment, and as he stared, the determined, efficient look left his eyes and was replaced by the one she had seen when he had first opened the door to Irene's house. It was a look of surprise, a look of delight. And it also held that strange panicky look that perturbed her so.

"I've been yelling at you, haven't I?" he said huskily. "When I should be telling you how lovely you look and how grateful I am that you're here. You could have made a fuss about coming, but you didn't. Do you know how wonderful you are?"

"Are you kidding?" she said, trying desperately not to sound as breathless as she felt. "I'll have you know I'm bordering on terrific."

He gave a soft laugh, then a devilish gleam

appeared in his eyes as he slowly placed his thumb in the valley between her breasts and hiked up the red dress.

"Let's go," he whispered, and ushered her into the large banquet hall.

Everyone was seated, and as they walked to the dais, James stopped to speak in a low voice to one of the waiters. By the time they reached their table, three men were arranging an extra chair and place setting.

Dempsey relaxed in her chair with a sigh and picked up her water glass. But before she could even take a sip she realized that James's hand and the silk scarf were also headed for her mouth.

James leaned toward her to whisper, "I think we'd better keep our hands under the table."

He moved their hands to her lap, but within seconds she knew that wouldn't work. His fingers were not still. As he clasped her hand in his, the back of his index finger moved gently against the lower part of her stomach.

She felt branded by his touch as shafts of heat flew to that spot. With a gasp, she moved their joined hands to his thigh. She could see his grin out of the corner of her eye, but she refused to acknowledge it. Instead, she picked up her water glass with her left hand and took a sip. At that moment, he tightened his grip on her hand and moved it to his lap, opening the fingers to press it close.

The people around them stared as Dempsey began to cough. When she was able, she looked up at James and smiled. It was a pleasant smile, a friendly smile.

But there were sparks of fire in her gray eyes. "You think that's amusing, do you? Just wait and I'll show you amusing."

The barely veiled threat didn't seem to bother him, but as they were served dinner he kept their hands resting modestly on his knee.

Dempsey managed all right with the fruit salad, but after she spent five minutes chasing English peas around her plate she gave up with a final wistful glance at her plate and simply waited for everyone else to finish. She noticed in irritation that James was eating every bite.

When the mayor finally introduced James as the main speaker for the evening, he gave Dempsey a rallying squeeze of the hand and together they walked to the podium. Luckily they were seated only a few feet from it and no one had time to question their joined hands.

Although Dempsey stood behind him, he could see the curiosity in the eyes that were trained not on him but on the woman behind him. There was nothing he could do but bluff it out.

He drew her forward until she stood beside him. "Before I get started, I'd like to introduce to you a citizen of our town who will shortly have some things to share with you that will be of great interest to everyone I'm sure." He turned to Dempsey. "Dempsey Turner-Riley."

She smiled and nodded her head graciously, trying to look studious and intellectual, then moved to stand behind him once again.

James took a sip of water, pulled his speech from

his breast pocket, then placed his right hand on the podium.

"I don't think the subject of my speech will be a great surprise to anyone. The thing that is foremost in our minds—and has been for some time—is the question of practical, if not legal, annexation of our city into Los Angeles." He paused. "I think you all know how I stand on this issue. If we are to progress, if we are to come into the twentieth century, we *must* be identified in the minds of prospective business residents and tourists with Los Angeles."

He opened his mouth to continue, then noticed that almost everyone in the audience was looking off to his left. He glanced down to find Dempsey had moved forward and now stood beside him. She cleared her throat.

"He's right," she said, nodding her head knowledgeably. "Of course, he's right. We need to be identified with Los Angeles. The problem is, how? What does the average person think of when they think of Los Angeles?" She paused. "I'll tell you. Weirdos." She smiled as though pointing out the obvious. "The average person expects to see strange people hanging around on the street corners when they come to Los Angeles. Remember, they can see normal in Idaho, but they come to California for weird."

She didn't seem to notice the titters and smothered laughter from the audience or the way James's eyes moved to the ceiling in silent supplication.

"I don't know much about the business end of this," she continued, "but surely we could place some kind of ad in the newspapers. Maybe we could appoint a committee to look into it. We're not looking for amateurs. What we need are big-league, heavy-duty weirdos." She glanced up at James, nodded briskly, then stepped behind him once again.

"Er—thank you, Ms. Turner-Riley," James said weakly, then turned his back to the audience and hissed, "What do you think you're doing?"

"I'm trying to help you out," she whispered back, her eyes innocent. "They obviously expect me to contribute something." When he remained silent, she added smugly, "Besides, I owe you. Remember?"

He stared down at her for a second, taking in the guileless look. "Now I know how Oppenheimer felt," he muttered before turning back to the audience that was beginning to get restless.

"As I was saying," he continued, "any business moving into the area would want to know that we were as forward thinking, as modern as the city of Los Angeles."

"Right," Dempsey said promptly, this time giving him no warning of her interruption. "You only have to look around to see what we're doing wrong. Consider our mayor." She lifted her left hand to indicate the clean-cut rotund man sitting on James's other side. "He looks much too normal." The laughter was a little louder now. "He looks intelligent and *sane*, for heaven's sake. C'mon, people, give me a break. He's so conservative, he wears a double-breasted bathing suit to the beach—with his *own* wife yet."

The rounded man in question seemed to be enjoying her comments as much as his neighbors were. The people sitting close enough were good-naturedly slapping him on the back.

"Now, consider the mayor of the town just south of here. Oh, don't moan. You all know who I'm talking about. Now, there's a mayor who's forward thinking and modern. He keeps a sheep for a house pet. You should see the size of his litter box. Are you kidding? We're talking major deviate here. Even his corn pads are leather. And what does our mayor do for relaxation?"

She glanced around expectantly, then shook her head in sorrow. "He collects stamps. If we called him a philatelist it might sound a little kinkier, but certainly some nut would look it up and the whole thing would be exposed. Think about it."

She gazed up at James and once again nodded solemnly before stepping behind him, this time to a round of applause.

"Thank you, Mr. Bones," James murmured in resignation. Pulling gently at his collar, James looked around the room and tried to retrieve the dignity with which his speech had begun.

"Another problem is our school system," he said hoarsely, then jumped nervously when Dempsey appeared beside him to say, "Schools!" in loud indignation.

The audience was already laughing in enjoyment before she could say another word, but she raised her hand to silence them as she shook her head. "We all know about the schools. They're a disgrace to any modern city." She leaned forward to speak confidingly. "Do you know what our girls look like?

Cheerleaders," she said in disgust. "Clean-cut, rosy-cheeked cheerleaders. And the boys—the boys are worse; they actually like *girls*. It's all so . . . so wholesome."

"Oh, what the hell," James muttered in resignation as he threw his speech into the air. To the accompaniment of loud laughter he bowed solemnly, then turned to indicate Dempsey, presenting her for applause and cheers before turning the podium over to the still-laughing mayor.

All through the mayor's closing speech James stared down at Dempsey and he knew the urge to strangle her was reflected in his gaze, but she merely stared at him with those big, innocent gray eyes.

As the applause for the mayor died away, people began to leave their seats and James urged Dempsey toward the door with a muttered, "Come on, for heaven's sake."

But before they had gone two feet, they were surrounded by a group of people and James was being heartily congratulated on his presentation.

"It was an inspiration, James. I couldn't have done better myself."

"I have to admit I was for annexation until I came here tonight. But you're right, James, completely right. It's not progress if we have to sacrifice the important thing—a good, decent place to live for our families."

"Wonderful, James, just wonderful. If you had tried to shove the facts down their throats, no one would have accepted it. But exaggerating what it would be like if we were part of Los Angeles was perfect."

As the crowd thinned, a small, intelligent man came up to stand beside him. He stared at James with a puzzled look in his eyes as they shook hands.

"You surprise me, James," he said quietly after he had been introduced to Dempsey. "Somehow I got the idea that you were for big business . . . at any price." He shrugged and smiled. "I'm glad I was wrong."

It soon became evident that they weren't going to leave quickly or quietly, and as others stepped up to speak to James, his smile became strained. His mind was quite obviously on something else, for he kept glancing at his watch and his dark eyes revealed his impatience.

When they managed to break away at last, he was muttering curses under his breath. Struggling to get into the car didn't help his disposition, and when they finally pulled away from the hotel, his distraction and irritation were apparent.

"Dammit to hell," he grumbled. "I wanted to get you taken care of before ten. There's no help for it. You'll just have to come with me."

"Is it all right if I ask where we're going?" Dempsey asked cautiously. "Since I'm driving, it might be a good idea for me to know," she added.

He was silent for a moment, then he turned to give her a grim smile. "We're going to meet a man in an alley."

Three

"Okay, you can pull over and park here."

"Here?" Dempsey echoed, glancing warily at the dark, deserted buildings lining both sides of the streets.

Although she didn't recognize the area, she could tell by the faded, worn storefronts that they were now in an older part of Los Angeles. Even the street lamps seemed tired, putting out just enough light to show that this was somewhere Dempsey would rather not be.

The few people on the streets—an old man who shuffled along, moving slowly from necessity rather than pleasure; a young woman, still wearing her waitress's cap and apron, who walked gingerly on painful feet; and groups of young, watchful men who hugged the shadows next to the buildings—all faded quietly into their surroundings.

As Dempsey pulled the car to the side of the street, she left the motor running to repeat in disbelief, "Are you sure you mean *here*?"

"I'm sure."

The distracted tone of his voice made it obvious James's thoughts weren't fully on her. Taking her hand with him, he reached over to switch off the engine, then without speaking opened the door on his side. He twisted sideways to plant both feet firmly on the sidewalk before helping Dempsey over the console and out of the car.

"James," she said thoughtfully as they walked along the shadow-streaked sidewalk, he with purpose, she with reluctance. "You—you never did mention exactly what it is you do for a living."

His laugh was quiet but abrupt as he glanced sideways at her. "Are you afraid you've become involved with an underworld character?"

She peered around again at the dubious quality of their surroundings. "You've got to admit most people don't go traipsing around in this part of the city by choice—unless they've got something to hide."

"Or unless they've got something to find," he murmured, his tone showing irritation. "It's a long story, Dempsey. Let's just say I'm being forced to play a rather childish game that I don't much care for."

She couldn't imagine James being forced to do anything he didn't want to do, but since he seemed in no mood for explanations, she didn't think it wise to press him. They had walked a block with Dempsey peering nervously into the shadows when James slowed his brisk pace, then, without comment, turned into an alley.

"This is it," he said quietly, and his voice echoed eerily in the heavily shadowed silence of the narrow lane.

"This is what?" she whispered skeptically. "It looks like a movie set for *I Was a Teenage Wino.*" She glanced around again, her nostrils twitching suddenly. "You know, the most interesting combinations of smells are lingering here. Sort of a mixture of wet dog, old sneaker, and new garbage."

He tried to keep his face straight as he pulled her closer and gazed down at her. "Nobody said it was the Ritz. How is an alley supposed to smell?"

"You've got me there," she admitted. "I don't think I've been in more than three alleys in my life, so I really shouldn't criticize when I'm not qualified to judge. This could be the top of the line as far as alleys go. You know—"

She broke off and jumped skittishly when a cat landed with a metallic thud on top of a garbage can. Inhaling to steady her nerves, she smiled. "Looks like we've been stood up," she said, her voice bright as she moved away from him, taking a backward step toward the entrance to the alley. "Gee, that's a real shame. . . ."

Her voice drifted off when her eyes focused on something in the shadows within the depth of the alley. "*James,*" she said in a shaky whisper, hastily gluing herself to his side as she nodded in the direction of the man who was beginning to take shape in the dark.

As they walked toward him, Dempsey dragged her feet. This was simply not her idea of a fun date. Then the man turned, and when the pale light struck his face she let out a sigh of relief. This was no gangland hit man. The stranger was thin and middle-aged and looked as nervous as she felt.

"Halloran?" the man said, his voice sounding cautious and habitually tired.

James nodded, then asked casually, "You have something for me?"

Dempsey stared at James in curiosity. He was trying not to show the stranger how anxious he was, but something about his face gave him away.

"You were supposed to come alone," the man said in irritation. Suddenly he spied the handcuffs and quickly began to back away. "What is this? Why are you handcuffed to her? Who is she anyway? What's going on?"

Dempsey moved forward and flashed open the lapel of the lace blouse. "Sergeant Saturday, Vice," she said, her voice and features bland. "You've got five minutes with my man, then I have to take him in."

"Dempsey," James said, pulling her back behind him. "Behave yourself and keep quiet."

"Or what?" she murmured dryly. "Or you'll make me wait in the car?"

"Look," James said, directing an impatient frown at the stranger. "Let's get on with this. Do you or do you not have something for me?"

"I ain't got nothing, man," the stranger said. "The

old broad told me to wait here in the alley and when you showed up *alone* to tell you . . . uh, let me see . . ." He closed one eye, his brow wrinkling as though he were trying to remember. "Oh, yeah, she said:

> Though it may sound incredi*bell*,
> Quixote is alive and well.
> So don't give up on what you seek,
> He'll be in touch again next week.

At least I think that's what she said," the nervous stranger added gruffly.

"Incredi*bell*," Dempsey murmured as she glanced at James in disbelief. "Incredi*bell*?"

"*Damn* him." James groaned, closing his eyes tightly in frustration. But it wasn't more than a second before he had control of his emotions and asked, "The 'old broad,' what did she look like?"

The stranger shrugged carelessly. "She looked like a hundred other old broads. Blue hair, thick shoes, and boobs down to her waist."

"Sounds like my agent," Dempsey said under her breath. "Except Murray's bald."

Ignoring her, James said, "Did you notice what color her eyes were? Did she have a masculine walk?"

"Look, James," Dempsey interrupted, "you really shouldn't pump this poor man. If he tells you too much, Mr. Big won't like it." She shook her head. "You know what would happen then. Stiff city."

"Mr. Big? You got somebody else in on this?" A sheen of perspiration appeared on the stranger's forehead. "The old broad didn't say nothing about

Mr. Big. And anyway, you can't . . . you can't pin a thing on me. I was just—"

"Dempsey, will you shut up," James said. She could feel his body shaking with silent laughter. Turning to the man, he said, "Calm down. There is no Mr. Big." He exhaled roughly, then glanced down at Dempsey. "This is useless. Let's get out of here."

"Hold on," the thin man said, moving after them as they walked toward the alley entrance. "The old broad said you would pay me, uh, twenty bucks . . . yeah, twenty bucks for waiting for you here and giving you the message."

"Twenty!" Dempsey said, her voice outraged. "James, don't do it." She stared stubbornly at the stranger. "We'll give you ten and you should be glad to get it."

"*Dempsey*," James said, pulling her arm behind her so that he could squeeze her waist in a warning to keep quiet.

"Don't give him a penny more than fifteen," she whispered. "The old broad has probably already paid him."

Reaching into his breast pocket, James pulled out his wallet and handed the man a twenty-dollar bill, then walked away, dragging Dempsey behind.

"Highway robbery." She was still muttering in disgust as she pulled the car away from the curb. "Why didn't you let me deal with him? I probably could have gotten him down to seventeen-fifty."

"I don't care about the money, Dempsey," he said. He sounded tired and frustrated.

"But he didn't have what you were after," she

argued. "It was just a ruse to make you more anxious. So you'll pay more for it when they finally do produce it."

He studied her silently, then said, "What in sweet heaven are you talking about?"

"That's exactly what happened in *The Indigo Caper.* Only they didn't get the golden bear back at all." She lowered her voice, throwing him a significant glance. "They *both* went down with the boat."

"Dempsey, I know what you're saying must make perfectly good sense to you," he said in exasperation, "but to me it's about as clear as mud."

"It's a movie I was in." She glanced at him in astonishment. "Don't tell me you didn't see it."

"I'm afraid I didn't."

"I said don't tell me," she muttered, then suddenly she grinned. "To tell you the truth, it wasn't a very good movie. In fact, it stank. It was released only three months ago and it's already on cable." She glanced across at him. "It will be on again Wednesday night."

"I'll be sure to watch it," he said dryly. "Turn here."

She turned the steering wheel to the right. "Well, if you do, you'll probably miss me. It wasn't what you would call an important part. But be sure and watch the credits. I'm listed as Girl in Mesh Bikini."

He studied her silently. "Are you an actress?"

"No, it was strictly from hunger, just like selling vacuum cleaners." She glanced around inquisitively. "Where are we going now?"

"There's an all-night superstore just around this

next corner." He nodded to the right. "I'll be able to buy a hacksaw there."

The parking lot of the superstore was brightly lit . . . an enormous relief to Dempsey after the dark alley. Inside the store, James went to the right while Dempsey quickly chose the left, then just as quickly changed her mind and decided to follow her hand.

James guided her impatiently toward the back of the store, where a large wooden sign proclaimed HARDWARE, pulling at her arm fiercely each time she paused to look at an item that caught her interest.

The hardware section was not an area in which James had spent a lot of time, and it took them a while to locate the aisle containing hacksaws. But eventually they found it and James reached out in relief to take one of the small, curved-handled saws.

"Naw, that's not whatcha need."

They swung around together to stare at the man who stood immediately behind them. He was big and bearded, his khaki uniform making it evident that he had spent a day doing rough, dirty work.

"I beg your pardon?" James said, raising one brow in aloof inquiry.

"The hacksaw. It'll take hours." When they merely stared at him, he said, "You wanna get the cuffs off, don't you?" He gestured toward their hands.

"Yes, sir, we do," Dempsey said, smiling.

Although James found it unbelievable, Dempsey didn't seem to notice the young couple who had stopped in the aisle to listen and stare curiously at their joined hands, but James wasn't able to ignore them so easily and began to shift in extreme embarrassment.

"Do you know how we could manage it?" Dempsey asked brightly, giving James a puzzled glance when she heard his low curse.

"Sure," the large man said with good-natured heartiness. "Whatcha need here is bolt cutters. They'll do the job just like that." He snapped his fingers. "That hacksaw, now, would take you forever. But bolt cutters—" He snapped his fingers again. "Just like that."

Leaning around them, he pulled a pair of cutters from the crowded wall display. James shifted his eyes to the ceiling and kept them there as another, then another late-night shopper stopped to watch.

"Here you go," the burly man said, handing the cutters to James. "If them cuffs was iron or something, a hacksaw'd be all right."

Reaching down, he grabbed their cuffed hands and held them up, apparently unaware of James's pained features. "But whatcha got here is stainless steel. You'd wear out a long time before the handcuffs did. You see if those bolt cutters don't fix you up. They'll do the job—"

"Just like that," Dempsey said, snapping her fingers. "Thank you so much for your help, Mr. . . .?"

When he saw a security guard stop at the end of the aisle and give them a hard, narrow-eyed stare, James leaned down to whisper, "Dempsey."

"Just call me Deke, ma'am. Everybody does. And I'm glad to help," he added affably. "Just hate to see people buy the wrong tools. Right tools'll last you a lifetime."

"Dempsey," James said more urgently. He could feel the heat creeping up his neck as he tried to urge her away from the growing crowd.

But she merely smiled at Deke in gratitude, as though they were on a pleasant Sunday outing and had all the time in the world. "Now the next time we get handcuffed together we'll have the proper tool," she said. "Thank you for taking the time to set us straight, Deke."

"Dempsey." James's desperation was obvious now. He swung her around on his free side, holding her tightly around the waist as he propelled her toward the front of the store then on to the checkout counter.

A shudder of relief shook him when they walked out of the store at last. How on earth had he gotten into such a crazy situation? Things like this simply didn't happen to James Halloran. He led an orderly, quiet life, and he liked it that way.

"What a nice man," Dempsey said as he hurried her across the parking lot toward the car. She glanced up. "Wasn't he a nice man, James?"

"He was a gem of a man," James said through clenched teeth, then, when he thought again of the security man, the crowd, and Deke, his lip began to twitch. It was no wonder she had taken the whole outrageous episode in her stride. Dempsey herself was outrageous. She probably felt right at home.

He glanced down at her to find her watching him with a mischievous sparkle in her wide gray eyes.

"You little devil," he murmured. "You did all of that intentionally, didn't you?"

"What will you do if I say yes?" she asked, eyeing him cautiously.

"I'll probably box your ears," he said, then began to laugh. "What am I going to do with you?"

"You could try releasing me from bondage," she suggested with an audacious grin.

Still chuckling, he raised their hands and brought them to rest on the top of the car. "Hold your hand steady. We'll get them separated now, but you'll have to go to a locksmith tomorrow to get the bracelet removed."

Then he applied the cutters. Deke was right. Two smooth cuts and the cuffs were divided. For a few minutes all James could think of was at last regaining control of his car and his life, then when he pulled out of the parking lot and Dempsey began to tell him where she had left her car, the truth hit him like a blow. This was it. They were free of each other and as soon as he returned her to her car, he would never see her again.

This was what he wanted, wasn't it? This was what he had been eagerly waiting for—to be free of her, to have his life return to normal. Then why did he suddenly feel empty and let down? he wondered with a frown.

It seemed impossible that he had met her only that very day. It went against all the rules of logic. In his mind, he knew her, really knew her. Logically he was aware that this kind of relationship simply couldn't be built in a few hours. And yet it had happened.

He felt somehow saddened to think that she would step out of his car and out of his life just as though they were strangers, just as though the closeness of the past few hours had never existed.

As he drove, a vision of her body—smooth white flesh above ridiculous purple bikini panties, a glimpse of small, perfectly formed breasts—flashed through his mind. He thought of her talking to Tim and Andy as though they were her equals. And of the way her crazy sense of humor crept into every situation. There should have been time for him to explore her, to explore the way she made him feel.

From the corners of his eyes he glanced now at the woman sitting next to him, studying her face, her small bow-shaped lips. It just didn't seem right that it should all end before he had a chance to touch her and taste her and learn the intricacies of her.

The plan he had tentatively formed earlier in the day, the plan to settle down and raise a family, nagged at him stubbornly and felt like an intrusion. He didn't want to think about stability and marriage. He wanted to think of Dempsey's lips against his. And plans or no plans, he wasn't committed to anyone yet.

As he forced himself to concentrate on the street ahead, he could feel her eyes on him, sense the confusion in her stare and knew he should try to make conversation. But what could he say? *Dempsey, I'm going to settle down soon, but could I have a last fling with you first?* Oh, Lord, was he so rotten a character?

He exhaled slowly, then reached over to pick up her

hand, staring straight ahead as he said, "Dempsey . . ." He didn't have to look at her to know he had her attention, but the words came with difficulty. "I was so eager to get the handcuffs off," he continued slowly, "but now that they are . . . now that they are, I think I miss your hand."

Silence filled the space between them like a solid wall, and James almost held his breath as he waited for her reply. He didn't ask himself why her response was so important to him. He didn't want to know right now. He couldn't think of anything beyond the moment.

When she spoke at last, her tone of voice was whimsical, her words slow. "It has been one very strange evening."

The tendons in the back of his neck relaxed a little. It wasn't exactly the response he had hoped for, but at least it showed she was aware of the unusual quality of the atmosphere between them.

"You feel it, too, don't you?" he asked, his voice rough with relief.

A small, wry smile twisted her lips. "You mean the feeling that we've just been left hanging in space?"

He nodded. "As though there's something unfinished between us."

Leaning down, she took off the gold slippers, wiggling her toes as she placed them in her lap. "I've been thinking about that," she said, her head cocked to one side as she gazed at him. "Couldn't it be that since we were inseparable, I observed and participated in your life—in intimate parts of your life—that I wouldn't ordinarily be privy to? The nature of our

dilemma forced us into an intimacy that's unnatural
. . . and probably artificial."

James frowned. It was a logical explanation, but he
ignored the logic. He focused on the fact that she was
obviously fighting the attraction between them as
much as he was and, unreasonably, the thought irritated him. He wanted Dempsey to be glad of it, even if
he couldn't be.

"We were forced into a closeness that wouldn't have
happened otherwise," she continued pensively, shaking her head, "but we don't know each other, not
really."

As he turned down the side street she had indicated, he spotted an old Volvo sitting at the curb.
Pulling up behind it, he switched off the engine, then
said simply, "It feels like we do."

"I know." She turned toward him and the vivacity
returned to her voice. "But that's a false impression,"
she said enthusiastically, as though they were having
a friendly debate. "I think after all we've been through
together our minds are having a tough time adjusting to the fact that we are virtually strangers." She
gestured with one of the gold shoes toward her head.
"It's like our brains are saying, 'So where do we go
from here?' "

He moved closer, staring down at her piquant
expression. "Where do we?" he asked, watching her
with an uncontrollable fascination.

Their eyes met and he felt as though a flame were
ignited in his head to spread liquid fire through his
body. Every nerve was vibrantly alive, and he knew
with absolute certainty his flesh would react with

pain to a simple touch, so sensitized had it become at the look in her eyes.

She moistened her lips nervously, then cleared her throat and murmured, "I guess the smart thing would be to say, 'It's been interesting, but now it's over,' then, um, then get on with our lives."

He reached up to touch her face, his thumb moving slowly across her cheek, then her lips, the feel of her sending urgent messages to his body. "Do you always do the smart thing, Dempsey?"

Dempsey couldn't keep her mind on what he was saying. He was so close now, she could feel his breath on her lips and see the fine wrinkles around his eyes. How could ordinary eyes be so patently sensual? She felt the hair on the back of her neck stand on end and inhaled roughly.

"Almost never," she admitted in a reluctant whisper, her eyes meeting his.

"Thank God." His words were almost a groan as he clasped her neck and urgently brought her lips to his.

It felt as though she had been waiting for this kiss forever, and Dempsey gave herself over to the pure pleasure of it. This is what she had wanted from the moment she first saw him, she realized incredulously. As crazy as it seemed, she felt that in his hands, in his lips, was the answer to the unknown question that had plagued her all her life.

Pulling her closer, James mentally cursed the console that kept them apart, his mind stunned by the explosion of sensation her lips brought. It was a feeling beyond anything he had ever experienced.

And as he became dazzled by the intensity of the pleasure, every thought in his head slipped away.

There was no future, no business, no Uncle Charlie, no Chloe. There was only Dempsey's mouth open to his, Dempsey's tongue seeking his, Dempsey's breasts pressed against him, the warmth of her thighs and stomach beneath his hand. There was only Dempsey.

"I wanted to do this the minute I opened the door this afternoon," he said, sounding surprised as he pushed the lace blouse off her shoulder to bring his lips to the flesh there. "It's the damnedest thing that ever happened to me," he murmured against her smooth skin.

Pushing her breasts up with both hands, he buried his face in the rounded flesh above the red dress. "This is not enough," he said, his voice hoarse. "You know it isn't enough."

"I know . . . *I know.*" She moaned against his lips, her body moving against his.

Abruptly he framed her face with hands he had to strain to keep still. "Come back to my apartment with me," he said. His voice was harsh and tight with suppressed passion. "Let me love you there, Dempsey. Let me love you right. I need to feel your body against mine. God, I want it so badly, my skin *hurts* from the want."

But he didn't give her time to answer. He couldn't stop himself from moving the fraction of an inch it took to once more find her lips. He couldn't get enough of her. He didn't want to stop touching her long enough to get back to his apartment. She was so warm, so willing, and he wanted it all. He had to have it all.

"Dempsey?" He breathed the question against her swollen lips.

"Yes," she gasped, nodding her head frantically. "Oh, yes, please."

He felt the relief of her answer run through his body. Giving her one last, lingering kiss, he moved away, leaning his head against the steering wheel, and slowly his breathing returned to normal. He had to get control of himself. This wasn't like him at all. He had never let logic be overwhelmed by emotion.

What is happening to me? he thought in the sizzling silence. His life was planned. He couldn't let a temporary physical attraction, no matter how powerful, disrupt it. He would make love to Dempsey, but he would keep his objectivity. He had to.

There was a simple explanation for what was happening, he told himself in desperation. Women like Dempsey normally weren't found in his circle. It was the novelty of her that was holding him in thrall. Of course, he assured himself, that was it. He was simply attracted to the difference.

His head jerked up when his intense concentration was interrupted by a startled sound from Dempsey. He turned to look at her and found that she was staring in chagrin at the digital clock on the dashboard.

"It's almost twelve," she said in disbelief. Raising her eyes to his, she added reluctantly, "I can't. I can't go with you." She bit her lip when it began to tremble. "I have to go to work."

She stared at him for a moment, her crooked smile

wistful. And before he could organize his chaotic thoughts she opened the door and said, "Tell Irene I'll return her dress and shoes when I pick up my equipment tomorrow." She paused. Then, her voice confused, she said, "Well . . . good-bye, James."

His hand came out to stop her before he had time to think. "Dempsey—" It was on the tip of his tongue to ask her to see him again, to beg her if necessary. But he stopped himself just in time. He curled his fingers into tight balls and held every muscle under control as he fought the words. He had to let her go. This small woman could get to be an obsession, and he simply couldn't afford to let that happen.

He could feel her eyes on him as he stared straight ahead. Finally, abruptly, he spoke.

"Good-bye, Dempsey," he said, his voice hoarse, then winced and closed his eyes when he heard the car door slam behind her.

Four

"Dammit, Uncle Charlie. Why are you doing this to me?" James raked his fingers through his hair, then turned back to look at the man seated before him. "You simply don't understand what you've done."

His uncle leaned his smooth, bald head back against the high-backed, brown leather chair that occupied the place of honor in the book-lined study of James's apartment. Charles MacGregor was a patient man. Years as a detective with the Los Angeles police department had taught him that. He folded his hands across his round stomach and studied his only nephew with infuriating serenity, not a single wrinkle showing on his smooth forehead.

"I probably understand more than you think I do,

son." Uncle Charlie's voice was soft and musical and, next to his blue eyes, was his most outstanding feature. "I understand that you're thirty-six and you have no family, no children, no *life* outside your work. It isn't natural. Don't you see that you're wasting your best years?"

He sighed, his eyelids drooping for just a second as though he were suddenly weary. "Someday, James, you're going to look back on these years and realize the truth of what I'm telling you." He opened his eyes to stare sadly at his nephew. "Then you're going to be hurt, and there won't be a blessed thing you can do about it."

"Uncle Charlie." James's angular face was set in lines of frustration and bewilderment. "You were dedicated to your work. You lived for the police department. Why is my work so different?"

"I was dealing with people, not facts and figures," his uncle said calmly. "I had human contact constantly and got human feedback—sometimes positive, sometimes negative, but it was always human. I was involved in life. You've very coolly, very deliberately, separated yourself from it."

James walked to the small fireplace and placed his forearms on the mantle, his fists clenched in anger. "I don't think we're just talking about people here. You're pressuring me to change my whole life and you picked an asinine way to do it. How is the loss of those papers going to show me that I need a wife and family?" He inhaled to control his anger. "And if I remember correctly, you've spent the better part of your life alone. What makes you an authority?"

His uncle leaned his head back against the smooth leather and closed his eyes. He remained silent for so long, James wondered if the old man had fallen asleep. When he spoke at last, his words were so soft, James had to move closer to hear them.

"I had two years with your Aunt Carey, James." He sighed in wistful regret. "Only two years, but I had enough loving in those two years to last me a dozen lifetimes. I don't know how to explain it to you. Separately Carey and I were only two people, but together we added up to *more*." He shook his head as though finding the explanation inadequate. "It's the memory of Carey that makes me keep at you like I do." His youthful eyes suddenly regained their usual twinkle. "Even when you want to disown me."

James sat down heavily, moved against his will by his uncle's words. This was no practical joke. Unconsciously James had known all along that there was more to it. Although he didn't understand, James was allowing his uncle to manipulate him because he sensed that the reason behind his charade was very important to the older man. "I've never wanted to disown you, Uncle Charlie," James said slowly. "It's mainly my concern for you that makes me so angry. I can't seem to get it through your head that you're in big trouble. The papers you took from my desk don't belong to me. They don't even belong to the company."

He shifted uncomfortably as he thought of the possible consequences of his uncle's foolish act. "Those papers were plans for a—well, it doesn't matter what they were for. All that matters is that those plans belong to an inventor, an individual. I merely had them to see if production and operation of the device were feasible. If it worked out right, then the company would have bought the patent, but"—he raised his voice now in irritation—"there was no chance to test it because you took the plans."

He turned to gaze earnestly at his uncle. "If I don't produce them soon, Uncle Charlie, we'll both end up in jail. You'll be arrested for theft, and they'll get me for aiding and abetting."

Although James watched his uncle's face for signs that his words had had an effect, the old man simply smiled indulgently, his sky-blue eyes sparkling with purpose. "Someday you'll thank me, James."

"Uncle Charlie, listen to me," he said in frustration. "You were a detective with the LAPD for *thirty years,* for heaven's sake. Doesn't it bother you to break the law like this? What you're doing doesn't make any kind of sense. You've only managed to disrupt my life and cause me a great deal of worry." He slapped his hand against his thigh, annoyed at feeling so completely helpless. "How can I get on with my personal life when all I can think about is what a mess you've made of my professional life?"

He stood up and went to kneel beside where his uncle was sitting. "Uncle Charlie," he said, speaking slowly, as though to a child, "I've decided that you were right about my needing a family." He smiled hopefully. "You see, none of this is necessary. I'm going to propose to Chloe tonight. In a few years you'll have my children as well as Irene's to spoil. So why

. . . why don't you just give me back those papers and we'll forget this ever happened?"

James watched his uncle in silence, praying that this time he had gotten through to him. A myriad of expressions crossed the round face before the older man spoke again.

"Chloe?" he asked doubtfully, then he frowned and shook his head slowly. "Chloe's nice, James. A real good woman. But you could marry her without even noticing." He slapped his hand against the arm of the chair emphatically. "No, she's not the one. Chloe would never make you angry enough to lose your temper."

James stared in confusion. "You want me to marry someone who will make me angry?"

Uncle Charlie chuckled in secret amusement, then stood up. "You're forgetting the other side of the coin." He nodded. "Someday you'll understand what I mean and, like I said, you'll thank me."

"You can't just leave it like that," James protested as his uncle walked down the hall toward the front door. "What about those papers?"

"I'll be in touch, m'boy," he said, slapping his nephew on the back. "I'll be in touch." Then the door closed softly behind him.

James swung around sharply, looking for something to punch. Why in hell did he need a woman to make him mad when he had Uncle Charlie? he wondered furiously. It took a good five minutes for his blood to stop boiling in his veins, then a glance at his watch showed he had only thirty minutes to shower and get ready for Chloe.

It took a major effort to force his thoughts away from his uncle and turn his mind to what lay ahead of him tonight. James had asked Chloe to have dinner at his apartment so that they could be alone. Tonight he would ask her to marry him, he thought decisively. Although the move was one he wanted to make for his own reasons, he couldn't help hoping when his uncle saw that he was engaged to be married, he would relent and return the papers he had stolen.

As he showered, James tried to imagine what his life would be like after he married. But the more he tried to think of Chloe, the more his thoughts turned to someone else—a small, volatile woman with a cocky manner and huge gray eyes. When he tried to call up Chloe's elegant blond good looks, he saw Dempsey's unruly black curls and her unorthodox manner of dressing. He tried to remind himself of how much he and Chloe had in common, but all he could think of was how Dempsey had made him laugh. And when he thought of making love to Chloe, it was Dempsey's lovely body that appeared in his bed.

He shook his head, full of self-contempt. If only he had brought her home that night, if only he had had the chance to make love to her, then he could have gotten over her. He smiled tightly. There was nothing like frustration to keep a man interested. Then he thought of her body, her mouth, the feel of her. It might have taken many, many nights to get Dempsey out of his system. There was something about her that pulled at him and made him want everything . . . and more.

He had to stop thinking about her, he told himself as he dressed. It had been a week since he had seen her, and the image of her hadn't diminished even though he knew he would never see her again.

Every time he thought he had succeeded in putting her out of his mind for a few minutes, something would happen to bring it all back. Irene had insisted on telling him in detail of how Dempsey had stopped by to collect the vacuum cleaner and had stayed for two hours to play with the kids.

Then on Wednesday, he could swear that it was by pure accident that he had found himself watching every minute of a very bad movie in order to find the girl in the mesh bikini. She hadn't been hard to spot. Even in a beach scene with dozens of bikini-clad women, Dempsey had stood out like an exotic, dew-covered tiger lily among wilting dandelions.

Stepping from the shower, James rubbed himself briskly with the towel, punishing his flesh for still wanting her. He would force himself to forget her. Thinking of her simply wasn't practical. Although he had introduced her as a citizen at the Chamber of Commerce dinner, he didn't even know if Dempsey lived in Sandley. There were hundreds of small towns in the Los Angeles area. It would be a major job even finding her telephone number.

Why in hell was he thinking about finding her? he wondered in dismay. He had everything planned—everything, down to the last detail—and Dempsey Turner-Riley wasn't a part of that plan. She was a complication he didn't need.

James had just finished combing his hair when the

doorbell sounded. Tonight, he thought firmly as he stared unseeingly into the mirror. Tonight he would propose to Chloe and get his plans under way once and for all.

"I'll get it, Mrs. Beckman," he called to his house-keeper as he walked to the entry hall.

His lips curved in a practiced smile as he opened the door to the tall, elegant blond woman. This was the type of woman James knew and felt at ease with. There was not a hair out of place in her smooth honey-colored pageboy. The pale blue dress she wore was elegantly understated, and her smile held just the right degree of detached warmth as he leaned down to give her a kiss of the same nature.

"You look beautiful," he said as he ushered her into the living room. "Sit down and I'll get you a drink," he said, walking toward the bar. "Dinner should be ready anytime now."

When he handed her a glass of the white wine she'd requested, James thought of how right Chloe looked against the background of his living room. Everything about her pointed to the fact that he had made the right decision. He sat down beside her on the couch, trying to relax as he listened to her quiet talk of Junior League luncheons and art exhibits.

This was his world and he felt secure in it, he assured himself silently. There was nothing here to agitate his mind or his emotions. This was where he belonged. This was what he wanted.

He frowned suddenly when he realized how hard he was trying to convince himself. Why did he have to think about it at all? Of course this was what he wanted.

". . . and then Sami said, 'Not really. But then I've been to Guadalajara.' James, are you listening to me?"

He shook away the nagging thoughts and smiled down at Chloe, forcing his full attention on her. But all through dinner, whether he wanted it or not, a small face with bow-shaped lips kept coming between them, disturbing his thoughts, cutting up his peace.

After Mrs. Beckman had removed the remains of their dinner to clear for dessert, his eyes took on a stubborn expression and he picked up Chloe's hand. He stared down at her long slender fingers for a moment, then exhaled slowly. He wouldn't put it off any longer, he told himself. He would do it now.

Dempsey leaned casually against the padded armrest that girdled the mirrored walls of the elevator and whistled along with the Muzak version of "The Girl from Ipanema." It was a nice song, but this kind of music always reminded her of the dentist's office.

She didn't need the various reflections around her to tell her this apartment building was not the kind of place she was used to, but she stared at her multiple images with an amused grin.

Several stubborn curls had escaped the French braid that hung down her back. The man's black sweatshirt she wore as a dress, the neck cut out so that it slipped over one shoulder, reached only to the middle of her thighs. The purple sash tied around her hips hung down to her knees and was the same color as her tights and leather ballet slippers.

She took off one shoe and rubbed her toes across the thick silver-gray carpet. James's apartment building was quite a contrast from her own. Most noticeable was the difference in smell. Her building usually smelled of meat loaf, baby powder, and Ben-Gay.

She chuckled at the contrast. This place smelled like the inside of a new Cadillac, but she would bet her socks that James never had to eat peanut butter and day-old bread in order to pay the rent.

Oh, well, she thought, shrugging in good-natured resignation. If she lived here, she would be a couple of years behind on the rent instead of only a couple of months.

When the elevator stopped on the twenty-third floor, she strolled casually down the hall, searching each door for 2311. When she found it she hesitated for a moment, then shrugged as she reached out to ring the bell.

He opened the door himself. "I'm impressed, James. I really am," she said as she walked past him. "Whatever business it is that you conduct in alleys in the dead of night must be ve-ry lucrative."

For a moment he looked as though she had hit him in the solar plexus with a sledge hammer, then that strange look of wistful longing crossed his dark, lean features as his eyes drifted slowly over her. But the expression was allowed to linger only a moment before his face became closed to interpretation.

Glancing away from him, she looked through a

curved archway and saw a tall blond woman sitting alone at a mahogany table laid for two. "You're having dinner," she said, meeting the irritation in his eyes.

"No one can accuse you of being slow," he said dryly as he closed the door behind her. "What are you doing here, Dempsey? How did you get my address?"

"Irene gave it to me. But we can talk later. You go ahead and finish your meal," she said over her shoulder as she walked into the dining room. "Hi," she said brightly to the woman seated there.

Dempsey heard James inhale slowly, then he said, "Chloe, this is Dempsey Turner-Riley, a . . . an associate of mine. Dempsey, this is Chloe Davis."

Dempsey stuck out her hand. "Pleased to meet you. You two get on with whatever you were doing," she said, her eyes shifting between the two of them as she smiled affably. "Just pretend I'm not here."

James exhaled a short breath and as she wandered around looking at the paintings on the walls she heard him speaking to his guest in a low voice.

"Don't worry about it, James," Chloe said. "I really don't want dessert. I can leave if you wish."

"But I wanted to talk to you," he protested.

She had begun to rise from the table, but when he spoke she paused. "Oh, of course. You were just about to say something when the doorbell rang."

"Is this painting real?" Dempsey asked without turning around. "The colors in it are wonderful."

James shot her an annoyed look. "Yes, it's real," he muttered, his gaze following her as she walked slowly from painting to painting. He couldn't take his eyes off her. She was audacious and impertinent, and he was totally fascinated by her uniqueness, he admitted ruefully.

"James."

He turned back to Chloe, his eyes bemused. Then he shook his head to clear it. "I'm sorry, Chloe. Did you say something?"

She smiled in amused exasperation. "*You* were saying something, remember?" she said. "You seemed to think it was important at the time, something about the fact that we have been dating for six months."

"Yes, of course," he said, amazed that his proposal had slipped his mind. "Actually—"

"Isn't it funny how when you hang around with someone for any length of time you get to look like that person?" Dempsey said as she walked closer to the two at the table. "For instance, Miss Davis smiles exactly the way you do, James. Isn't that weird?"

"*Dempsey.*"

"Oh, sorry." She grimaced in apology. "Go ahead, James, what were you going to say?"

He made a strangled noise in his throat, then, with heated deliberation, sent her an evil look. This was probably the look he used on Irene's children, Dempsey thought. But it had no more effect on her than it did on them. When she had gone to Irene for James's address, Uncle Jamie was all the three older children could talk about. And Irene was just as bad, Dempsey thought, remembering the way James's sister had talked on and on about him, telling her what a wonderful man he was and how he secretly longed for children and a family.

Dempsey was experienced enough to know an

attempt at matchmaking when she saw it, but in this instance it surprised her. Surely Irene could see that Dempsey and James were so totally different that they would have difficulty just being friends.

She hadn't disillusioned Irene during her visit. She could see how much the other woman cared for her brother, and it touched something deep inside Dempsey, reminding her once again of how much she had missed by being an only child. As she had watched Irene's children she had known that not only did she miss the companionship of siblings, she had missed out on the constant fun, the aliveness of a group.

The memory of the kids made her laugh aloud now, and James sent her a questioning look.

"What's funny?" he asked, smiling simply because she was. From the corners of his eyes he had watched her features as she stood quietly thinking. Her face was more alive than any he had ever seen.

"I was just thinking of Mikie," she said, still chuckling as she gave him a significant look. "He finally produced the key."

Leaning back in the chair, James's eyes sparkled with amusement. "Did he?"

"Yeah," she said, nodding. "And got a bigger round of applause than I've ever gotten." She shook her head. "There's simply no justice in the world."

He laughed uninhibitedly, the sound filling the room with warmth, then suddenly James remembered that he was annoyed with her. Shaking his head ruefully, he turned back to the other woman. "Chloe—" he began apologetically.

"Now I know who you remind me of," Dempsey said, snapping her fingers as she stared at Chloe. "Joe Epper. It's something about the eyes and forehead. Do you think he could be a relative?"

Chloe looked amused and bewildered as she glanced from James to Dempsey. "I don't think so," she said quietly.

"That's too bad. He's a super guy." She leaned against the paneled wall, raising her foot to scratch her ankle. "He played the green grapes in the underwear commercial. Maybe you've seen him?"

"I'm sorry," Chloe said politely. "I didn't notice the grapes."

"Poor Joey. Not many people do," she said sympathetically. "The apple gets all the attention. I wonder why."

James's lips twitched uncontrollably as he gazed at her. "It's the way of the world," he said, his eyes crinkling at the corners. "Apples get the glory while grapes are just quietly noble."

"Is that what it is?" Dempsey asked, grinning at him in appreciation, then she shrugged. "Oh, well, he made good money on that commercial."

"Are you in show business, Dempsey?" Chloe asked, laughter sparkling in her eyes.

"You could say that." She grinned suddenly, her eyes mischievous. "Murray, my agent, doesn't say that, but you could. He always—"

"Dempsey," James muttered in frustration.

She winced in chagrin. "I'm interrupting again."

Chloe laughed. "Why don't we talk tomorrow,

James . . . after you've finished your business with Dempsey."

"Don't let me run you off," Dempsey protested sincerely as the other woman pushed her chair back. "I wanted to ask where you bought those shoes. They're gorgeous. Not that I'd be able to afford them," she added with an unconcerned smile. "Shoes come right after meat, which is nineteenth on my list of what to buy when I get extra money."

Chloe stood up. "I really do have to leave now, Dempsey," she said with an amused smile. "Maybe we can talk some other time."

James walked her to the door and it was only seconds later when he reentered the room, a vengeful fire growing in his dark eyes.

"I really do like Clara, James," Dempsey said, smiling up at him. "I wish she could have stayed longer so we could talk."

"Chloe. Her name is Chloe," he said between clenched teeth. "Dempsey, I could—" He took a deep breath. "Now you can explain why you are here."

She shrugged, calmly studying his flushed face. "You're not going to believe it."

"Try me."

She leaned her hip on the polished sideboard. "The man from the alley gave me a note for you."

"What are you talking about?" he asked in frustrated confusion. "How did he find you? And why on earth would he give you a note for me?"

"James," she said dryly, "the man didn't stay to chitchat. He simply came to the club where I work— you know, he sure sweats a lot," she added in a wry aside. "He gave me this note and told me it was for you." She handed him a small, sealed envelope, then turned to leave. "So now I've done my duty and can leave."

James looked down at the envelope without opening it. His mind was in a chaotic turmoil. He felt torn in two different directions at once and he didn't know how to handle it. He had been so annoyed with her for interrupting his dinner with Chloe. But now he didn't want her to leave. Seeing her again was even worse than the first time.

"Wait, Dempsey," he said, hearing the urgency in his voice as he followed her into the hall. He felt uncomfortable and embarrassed when she turned to gaze at him inquisitively. "Would you—would you like a cup of coffee or a drink?" he asked lamely.

"Thanks, but I'd better not," she said, then glanced down at the envelope in his hand. "Aren't you going to read the note?"

"In a minute," he said shortly. He began to move closer to her, mesmerized by her nearness in a way that baffled him. "Dempsey, I can't stop thinking about you," he blurted out before he could stop himself.

She tried to hide an amused smile but didn't quite succeed. "How annoying for you."

"Don't laugh at me." He rubbed the back of his neck. "Every night while I lay in bed I think about what happened between us. And it's not getting better; it's getting worse." He glanced at her in consternation. "It's beginning to interfere with my work."

"Surely not," she said in horrified tones.

"This is serious." He began to pace back and forth in agitation. "I've got to get you out of my mind so I can get on with my life."

She studied him for a moment. "And how do you propose to do that?"

"You don't need to ask that. You know what I'm talking about." Slowly he reached out to touch her face. The feel of her skin dazzled him, making him lose all reason. "You're here now. Can't we pick up where we left off?"

She understood him perfectly. He wanted to make love to her—now that it was convenient. A pain struck somewhere deep inside her, but she ignored it. She knew what kind of man James was and she knew what he wanted from her. She had known the last time, but when he touched her it didn't seem to matter.

She wouldn't let it happen again, she told herself. She would be strong. She refused to let this man affect her.

She started to pull away, then suddenly his lips were on hers and a gasp of surprise escaped her. She had forgotten. She had put from her mind the help-lessness she felt when he kissed her. This was not something she could fight. This was life. This was the air she breathed. All her doubts, all her objections, slid into nothing under the force of his kiss.

She tasted his lips, inhaled the scent of him as though she had been starving for them. She could feel the desperate need in his every touch, and it was like lighting a fuse to dynamite.

She never knew how they got to the couch in his living room. Or how her dress came to be around her waist. She only knew she would die for the feel of his mouth on her breasts, his hands between her thighs.

"You're dangerous," he rasped, burying his face between her breasts. "I want to hold on to you and never let you go."

He didn't mean it. She knew he didn't mean it. She was old enough to recognize lust. But perhaps not wise enough to handle it, she thought suddenly.

When she became still he rose up to look at her. Avoiding his eyes, she moved back into the couch, away from him, and sat up.

"Dempsey?"

Sliding past his feet, she stood up, clutching her dress to her breasts. "I'm sorry," she whispered, and began to straighten her clothes.

She knew what making love to her would mean to James. It would mean nothing more than a night's amusement. And for one drugged moment she had thought that would make it all right. Nothing serious, just a short, casual affair. But Dempsey had forgotten to take into account what it would mean to her. It didn't feel casual. Inside her, deep inside her, it felt serious. And that was something she couldn't handle.

"Dempsey?" he said again.

She couldn't look at him. If she did, she would see that yearning and she would be lost. It wasn't fair that he could twist her insides with a single look.

"Isn't the mind funny, James?" she said, unaware of how vulnerable she sounded. "You're going along fine, thinking you're in control, then suddenly your brain steps in and throws everything into chaos." She shook her head. "If there's one thing I can't stand, it's a smart-aleck brain. It'll mess you up every time."

"What's your brain telling you now?" There was a gentleness, a tender quality about his voice that shook her to the core.

"It's saying 'Get the hell out of here,' " she said ruefully.

He stood up and reached out to turn her face toward him, forcing her to look at him, to see the aching desire that showed plainly in his eyes. "I don't suppose you could just tell it to shut up."

She laughed shakily. "I don't think so."

Then suddenly as she stared into his eyes, the softness began to disappear in one of the disquieting mood shifts she was beginning to associate with him. Suspicion began to grow in his eyes and with it anger. For long, tense moments he was silent, and she could almost feel his muscles grow taut with this new emotion.

Suddenly he turned, pinning her with blazing dark eyes. "This is the second time, dammit," he said tightly. "What are you trying to do to me?" He swung away from her, running a hand through his hair in frustration. "It was bad enough last time. I can only imagine what it will be like now."

She studied his face carefully, taking in the white line around his sensuous lips, his thin, flaring nostrils, then she said slowly, "I know this"—she waved her hand toward the couch—"was partly my fault, but be fair and remember who started it, James."

His eyes narrowed as though he didn't like being reminded. "But you were perfectly willing to go along with it. What made you change your mind? Do you want money?"

For a moment, fury exploded in her brain, showing in her eyes as they turned steel gray. Then just as suddenly it dissolved and irrepressible laughter took its place. "James," she said, tilting her head in inquiry, "are you calling me a prostitute?"

"*No*—" he began emphatically. Then a dumbfounded expression began to grow in his eyes. He rubbed the back of his neck and said in shock, "Good Lord, I think that's exactly what I was doing."

The anger was gone now and he sent her a look heavy with regret. "That was inexcusable," he said, disgust in his voice. "I'm sorry, Dempsey. Please stay. Let me make it up to you. We'll just talk," he added hastily when she looked at him skeptically.

"I can't," she said, pausing to straighten her sash. "I have an early show." She smiled, her eyes sparkling with amusement. "Don't worry about it, James. I'm not going to throw myself in the river. I've been insulted by better men than you. I'm like rubber; I bounce."

He knew he deserved her contempt, but that didn't stop his lips from tightening in reaction. Let her go, he told himself. She was trouble with a capital T. Somehow she made him do things that were completely unlike him. What in hell was the matter with him anyway? he wondered as guilt flooded him, bringing a tinge of red to his dark face. If Dempsey hadn't shown up, he would have proposed to Chloe, he would have made a vow to be faithful to her for the rest of his life. But he couldn't even be with Dempsey for one hour without trying to get her in bed. Yes, he thought in grim determination, he would let her go and his life would return to normal.

"Where do you work?" The words were out of his mouth before he could stop them, and James inhaled in surprise. He hadn't meant to speak at all. When she glanced back at him, he added defensively, "In case I need to get in touch with you about the note."

She opened the front door. "At the Green Duck, but I'm there only at night." She walked into the hall, then added over her shoulder, "Usually from ten until three in the morning, but sometimes earlier."

As he followed her into the hall, his brow creased in thought. "The Green Duck? Isn't that a strip joint?"

She nodded in distraction, glancing down at her watch. "Oh, dear heaven! I'll never make it in time. Murray will kill me. 'Bye, James."

She stepped quickly into the elevator and missed the stunned expression on his face as he watched the doors close between them.

Five

"Dempsey, have you seen my pink headband?"

Turning away from the mirror, Dempsey smiled at the woman standing behind her, hiding her amusement as she took in the shocking-pink fake fur coat and matching spike-heeled shoes. She had never been able to figure out how Mona could get away with wearing that particular shade of pink with her brilliant auburn hair. It should have been offensive to the eye, but somehow it wasn't.

"I'm sorry, Mona," she said, shaking her head. "Have you asked Kenny?" She motioned toward a plump young man who was at the moment digging through a pile of costumes.

"He hasn't seen it either," Mona said in a wail. "You

know I can't go on without my headband. It pulls my whole act together."

Giving her a sympathetic smile, Dempsey turned back to the mirror and met a pair of twinkling blue eyes.

"Do you suppose anyone ever really notices the headband?" the bald man behind her whispered as he glanced after the departing Mona.

Dempsey laughed, then leaned closer to continue applying her third coat of black mascara. "Probably not," she admitted. "But she's always afraid she'll look tacky. Mona likes to be coordinated."

"Shall I tell her how elegant she looks without any ornamentation at all?"

"It might help," she said doubtfully, and watched as her friend Mac crossed the small room to talk to Mona.

Mirrored vanities lined the walls; and the smell of makeup and nervous excitement clung to the air. With every passing second, the voices of the occupants became a little louder, a little shriller. The cluttered dressing room was shared by six women every night, and it tended to get a little wild when everyone started looking for costumes at once.

The only exception was Charlene, a veteran entertainer, who sat calmly smoking a long, thin cigarette as she applied her makeup, looking as though she had never heard of sweaty palms before a performance.

Dempsey grimaced. Staying calm in this atmosphere was difficult even if you could find all the pieces to your costume, which didn't happen very often. But if anyone could pacify Mona, it was Mac.

Dempsey had met Mac six months earlier in a coffee shop near the club where she worked. What had begun as a pleasant, impersonal conversation had turned into a warm, real friendship. She had been instantly attracted to the twinkle in his blue eyes and the old-world charm in his smile. And perhaps the fact that he was only six inches taller than herself added to the attraction.

Since then he had caught almost all of her shows and their friendship had grown. Mac always made her laugh. Although there was a big difference in their ages, it was a difference that was ignored by each of them.

Dempsey smiled when she thought of the mystery Mac made of how old he was. She had asked him about it once early in their friendship, but he had merely told her in a lofty tone that if she wanted to know, she would have to saw him in half and count the rings.

"She decided to use a pink ribbon," Mac said when he returned to her side a few minutes later. "Now, tell me, have you found another job?"

She shook her head. "And that reminds me." She eyed him sternly in the mirror. "What on earth made you think I would be able to sell vacuum cleaners in Sandley? The place was dead. Especially at five o'clock. I've got to be the world's worst salesman and even I—if I had stopped to think about it—would have known that five o'clock in the evening is not the time to approach people with vacuum cleaners. They're all dead tired at that time of day."

"You must have misunderstood me."

"Mac," she said, turning to face him, "you said as plain as day 'Go to Marlboro Street in Sandley on Wednesday at five o'clock.' What's to misunderstand?" Her eyes narrowed as she regarded him suspiciously. "Now that I think of it, the whole thing was pretty weird. What do you know about door-to-door sales anyway?"

"I hear things, my dear. I hear things," he said, giving a casual wave of his hand. "And I happened to hear that Marlboro Street in Sandley was an excellent place to sell vacuum cleaners."

"On Wednesday at five o'clock?" she asked, tilting her head to give him a doubting look. "Did you also hear that that was the best time to sell?"

He smiled guilelessly. "Didn't I tell you I was into numerology? According to the numbers, you should have made a killing then."

"Your numbers stink," she said bluntly. "Remind me not to take you to the track with me."

"Well, it doesn't matter," he said, waving the past away with an airy twist of his hand. "I've decided I'm not really keen on numbers anyway."

"I wish you had decided that *before* I lost my job," she grumbled, turning back to the mirror.

"You'll find something else. You're bright and intelligent. There must be thousands of jobs like that one just waiting for you," he said, dismissing her financial problems as too trivial to be of interest. "But in the meantime, tell me who you're dating now."

She gave him a sideways, wary glance. "Mac, you're not going to try to fix me up with your upwardly mobile nephew again, are you?"

"Dempsey," he said, sighing heavily, "you're not looking at this objectively. If you date my nephew, think how many meals you won't have to buy."

She turned to face him, placing her hands firmly on his shoulders. "Mac, you're a darling and I appreciate your efforts, but why would a rising young executive be interested in me?" She frowned. "And besides, they're so *boring*. All they can think about is how absolutely wonderful they are at their jobs. I couldn't possibly have anything in common with your nephew." She grinned. "And anyway, I'm growing rather fond of butter and stale bread."

He studied her for a moment. "It's that 'serious' business again, isn't it? You're afraid of someone like my nephew who takes life seriously, so you hang around with a bunch of goof-offs and dizzy-brains."

"I hang around people I have something in common with," she insisted stubbornly. "If they're goof-offs and dizzy-brains, then so am I."

"You're not, you know." He smiled a secret smile. "But I won't push it. Things usually have a way of working out for the best."

She eyed him suspiciously. "I don't trust you. What are you plotting?"

"You wound me, Dempsey darling." He kissed her cheek affectionately. "Break a leg, my dear. I'll be at my usual table."

Dempsey shook her head and laughed as he walked away, then turned back to the mirror to finish applying her makeup. Mac was a scheming old man, but he was a dear and she knew he only wanted her to be happy. She would just have to find a way to convince him that becoming involved with a man like his nephew would not guarantee her happiness.

A man like James, she thought, frowning suddenly. James had a way of popping into her head when she least expected it. The episode on his couch the night before had thrown her off her stride, and she knew her performance last night hadn't been up to par.

Her chin stiffened in determination. That would change. She wouldn't continue to let a total stranger upset her life. She would forget about James Halloran, she vowed as she began to shove her long hair up under the cobalt blue jockey cap that completed her costume.

"Dempsey, do y-you have time to talk?"

Dempsey turned to smile at the chubby teenager standing beside her. "You know I always have time to talk to you, Kenny." She hopped up on the vanity counter and rested her chin in the palm of her hand. "So tell me, how are the diction lessons coming along?"

"F-fine, I think. M-Mr. Michener says that I've made p-progress," he said proudly, then he seemed to sag. "B-but that doesn't really mean anything. I didn't have anywhere to go b-but up."

She laughed at his disgruntled expression. "Don't give up. You've got a lot of talent, Kenny. You have to believe in yourself."

"S-sometimes I do. When I think ab-about what I can do." He glanced at her shyly through the thick lenses of his glasses. "You s-see, I don't s-stutter in my head."

"I know," she said, reaching out to hug him. "But someday you'll be living it for real, not just in your head." She grinned. "I've told you what I was like when I was your age. If I can do it, then so can you."

He nodded. "T-that's what I keep telling myself. B-but I don't think I'll ever b-be a star like you." He gazed at her with unadulterated adoration.

Dempsey didn't laugh and she didn't correct him. To Kenny she was a star, and if he needed someone to be a role model, she was more than willing to play the part until he moved on to a real star.

"Sure you will," she said enthusiastically. "You just wait. As soon as you get that stammer taken care of, the talent scouts will be beating your door down. Then when you're rich and famous, you can buy Caesars Palace for me out of your pocket money."

He laughed heartily, obviously enjoying the picture she painted of his future.

This was all he needed, she thought, watching him with pleasure. Someone to make him laugh. Someone to show him that his speech defect wasn't an insurmountable obstacle. When you were eighteen with a stammer and a bad complexion, you had to have something to grab on to. Dempsey remembered only too well what it was like to be in that bleak position. The lack of money wasn't nearly as important as the lack of a friend to hold your hand when things were bad.

"Kenny, honey," a tall, raven-haired woman said, leaning close to the chubby young man. "If you could find my red boa for me, I would be ever so grateful."

When she leaned down to kiss his cheek, Kenny

turned a vivid shade of red. Taking off his glasses, he wiped at them nervously. Then with a bemused smile spreading across his face, he rolled his eyes at Dempsey and followed the woman across the room.

Dempsey smiled. She really liked the people she worked with. Once they had discovered how sensitive and shy Kenny was, each in her own way set out to make him feel comfortable. In an unspoken agreement they worked to make him feel important and even attractive, flirting with him innocently to build up his self-confidence.

Turning back to the mirror, she wondered idly what her life would have been like if she hadn't felt compelled to go into show business. She probably would have married an earnest young man and had dozens of earnest young children, she thought with a grin.

No, she decided, she wouldn't have married. She would probably have taken a secretarial course so that she could put up with the whims of an ambitious executive. And she would probably have ended her career by murdering her boss. She simply couldn't see herself in close contact with that type of man. Someone like Mac's nephew . . . someone like James.

Damn, she swore silently in exasperation. What was he doing back in her head? Was she never going to be rid of the memory of him?

Stubbornly pushing the thought of him away, she leaned closer to apply lipstick, then when the back of her neck began to tingle crazily, she raised her eyes in the mirror—to find the very real reflection of the man she had been trying so hard to forget.

Swinging around in surprise, she said, "What on earth are you doing here?"

But James's attention wasn't on Dempsey. His dazed eyes followed a woman who wore only a red bra, red bikini panties, and a black garter belt as he said in a faint, distracted voice, "I need to talk to you."

"Dempsey," a velvet voice cooed from across the room. "You've been holding out on us. He's *gorgeous*. Didn't your mother teach you to share with your friends?"

Dempsey hid her smile when she saw James's neck turn red. "I don't think Henry would like that, Candy."

"Henry? Who's Henry?" the voluptuous blonde replied with exaggerated innocence.

"Hey, baby girl, can I have him when you're through?" asked a plump, jolly-looking brunette dressed in a full-length white satin evening gown.

At that moment Charlene left her dressing table, giving the occupants of the room a good look at her long legs as they extended from a yellow, marabou-trimmed teddy, and moved gracefully across the cluttered floor to stand very close to James.

"Sugar," she murmured seductively in his ear, "when you get tired of playing in the minor league come see me"—she raised a finger and ran it down his nose and lips—"and I'll show you how we do it in the major league."

Dempsey laughed as Charlene winked and turned to walk out of the dressing room. "Don't pay any attention to them," Dempsey said, glancing at James's bedazzled expression. "They like to kid me."

James switched his gaze back to Dempsey, taking in the white satin knickers and the skimpy blue and white silk T-shirt. "Do you . . . do you enjoy your work?" he asked, studying her with the oddest look in his eyes.

"Enjoy?" she repeated, her brow creasing in thought. "I guess so. But that's like asking if I enjoy breathing. It's a part of me that I can't imagine living without." She gave him an inquisitive look as she stepped into her shoes. "Don't you feel that way about your work?"

He nodded slowly. "Yes, but I never thought about people taking this kind of thing"—he indicated the room with a wave of his hand—"seriously." He paused and studied her with curiosity. "Doesn't it bother you at all?"

"Doesn't what bother me?"

"All those people . . . watching you."

"That's why I'm onstage," she said, chuckling. "If they didn't watch me, I would be out of a job." When he remained silent, she added, "I'm not a shy person, James. I've seen you only twice, but I thought you knew that."

"Of course I knew. But this is different."

She gazed at him in growing bewilderment. He sounded almost angry. She knew there were a lot of people who looked down on anyone in show business, but she hadn't thought James was that type.

"If you don't like where I work, maybe you'd better

tell me what you came to say, then leave before any of it rubs off on you," she said dryly.

He massaged the back of his neck, his expression betraying his confusion. "No . . . no, it's not that. It's just that you don't seem the kind of person who would . . ." His voice died away.

"Who would *what*?" she asked in exasperation.

"Oh, I don't know," he said, obviously irritated. "Don't you ever get cold?"

It suddenly dawned on her what he was thinking and she held her hand to her mouth as laughter spilled out of her. "Oh, James. You're so very *p-proper*."

"What in hell's so funny?"

She tried to keep a straight face as she said, "Last night you thought I was a hooker and today you think I'm a stripper." Swallowing her laughter with difficulty, she said seriously, "I'm not a stripper, James. I'm a comedienne. I go on between acts." She looked up at him, frowning suddenly. "But if I was, I'd be a very good one . . . and I wouldn't let anyone put me down for it."

"That's not what I was trying to do," he said earnestly. "I was just surprised, that's all." He stared at her silently for a moment, his eyes drifting down her body, then said quietly, "Now I don't know whether I'm relieved or disappointed." He inhaled deeply, then stared at her straight in the eyes. "Dempsey, I'm sorry about last night. There was no excuse for what I said to you."

Her body reacted to his examination as though it were his hands on her rather than his eyes. She wished he would go away and leave her alone. He was disrupting her life more than she had ever allowed anyone to disrupt it.

"You apologized last night," she said, glancing away from him. "There was no need for you to come all this way to do it again." She paused, staring at him in speculation. "Unless there was another reason for your visit."

He was silent for a moment, looking vaguely uncomfortable, then he exhaled roughly and said, "That note you brought last night contained instructions on how I can get back something that was stolen from me. Something that I need badly."

She swung her gaze back to his face, wondering why he had come to find her just to tell her this. It had nothing to do with her.

Meeting her expectant gaze, he clenched his fists and said tightly, "The note said the papers won't be turned over to me unless you're with me."

Her eyes widened in astonishment. "That's crazy. How would someone involved in your work know about me? We met only last week." She glanced at the clock on the wall. She would have to go on in moments. She simply didn't have time for this now. "I wouldn't worry about it," she said, her voice distracted. "It's most likely some kind of practical joke."

"Dempsey," he said, following her out of the dressing room, "this is no joke."

But she didn't hear him. Her mind was already on the performance ahead of her as she stood to the side of the stage. It was always the same. She felt a giant fist close around her stomach, her heart started jerking in her chest, her hands began to shake, and she felt as though only her iron constitution kept her from throwing up.

Just when she felt like she couldn't take any more tension without going crazy, she heard the announcer's bright, overenthusiastic voice.

"And now, coming fresh from her smash appearance in Las Vegas, ladies and gentlemen, I give you our own . . . *Dempsey Turner-Riley!*"

Drawing in a deep breath, she skipped onto the stage, her arms spread wide in a welcoming gesture. She moved into the spotlight and the reality of the audience hit her like a solid thing, lifting her up, turning her into someone else—someone familiar, but not the person who climbed into her narrow bed each night.

James had followed Dempsey from the dressing room impatiently and now stood at the side of the stage watching her perform. After a moment he forgot that he was annoyed with her and became totally absorbed in her act.

It was immediately apparent that Dempsey was not a run-of-the-mill one-liner comedienne. She sat on a stool with a coffee cup in her hand and pretended to be talking with a friend. At first the audience seemed not to notice her, her words just audible over the rumble from the club. But little by little the talking died down and the patrons closest to the stage were joined in laughter by the ones in the back.

There was something truly unique about Dempsey and her act. James felt as though he were eavesdropping on an enthusiastic, slightly bawdy gossip session. She poked fun at adultery, bigotry, and jealousy. And by exaggerating those things, she showed them in their true light. She made a substantive person think without making the lighthearted uncomfortable. And no matter what the personality of the listeners, they laughed.

Perspiration and exhilaration were shining on her face when she walked off the stage at last, the sound of enthusiastic applause following her. Mona handed Dempsey a towel as she passed. "You were great, baby girl," she said over her pink fur-clad shoulder.

"Thanks, Mona," she said as she wiped her face. "Good luck," she added as the blond woman made her way onto the stage. Then she saw James and her eyes widened in surprise. "Are you still here?"

He stared down at her, a bemused expression softening his angular features. "You were wonderful."

She laughed. "Why do you sound so surprised? I told you I was terrific."

" 'Bordering on terrific,' " he corrected her softly, a reminiscent smile on his face. "And it was an understatement, believe me. Have you really appeared in Las Vegas?"

"That's an old joke," she said, chuckling. "About a year ago I was working as a waitress at a restaurant on Las Vegas Street. They fired me because I broke six glasses in my first—and last—hour on the job." She smiled up at him. "So—smash appearance."

When she started to walk past him, he grasped her arm. "Dempsey, we have to talk. I want—"

He broke off suddenly, his expression stunned as he stared at something behind her. Puzzled, Dempsey glanced over her shoulder to the brightly lit stage where Mona was in the middle of her dance.

"They're— It's— Everything's *pink*," he sputtered in quiet astonishment.

She nodded. "Mona likes to be coordinated."

He shook his head dazedly, then glanced back at her. "Look, I really need you to come with me tomorrow."

Oh, no, she thought warily. Not again. She couldn't even consider going with him. He didn't know how much power he had over her and she wasn't about to give him another chance to find out. The man was dangerous.

Every time they touched, an emotional explosion occurred inside her. Dempsey was not self-destructive. Years of living alone had taught her to be wary of anything that threatened her well-being. James was definitely a threat—to her emotional security, to her work. And she wouldn't chance harming her career for anyone.

Moving away from him toward the dressing room, she shook her head in determination. "I can't."

He stared at her retreating figure. "You mean you won't," he called after her.

"Okay, I won't," she agreed, shrugging, then glancing over her shoulder, she said, "Why can't you get Claudia to go with you?"

"Chloe," he corrected absently. "She won't do. The note said it had to be you." He sighed and three long strides brought him even with her. "Dempsey, I made an ass of myself last night." He frowned. "It's not something I like remembering. I promise it won't happen again." When she remained silent he said, "I said those things out of spite only because . . . because I got a little carried away."

She stopped walking and turned to stare up at him. "What you said doesn't bother me. Maybe it did a little at the time," she admitted honestly, "but not anymore. It's the 'carried away' part that is bothering me. It happens every time we're together."

"This will be strictly business," he assured her earnestly. "I promise."

She frowned, unwilling to be swayed by the sincerity she heard in his voice. "I don't know," she murmured reluctantly, then shook her head and began to walk away from him.

But she couldn't resist a small glance in his direction, and that glance proved to be her undoing. His lean face was held in stern lines, reminding her of a studious schoolboy who kept to his books while others played. Suddenly she wanted to smooth away those sober lines and replace them with lines of laughter.

And why not? she debated silently. It couldn't take that long to retrieve the papers. Why make such a big deal of it? A small wry smile twisted Dempsey's lips as she forced honesty into her calculations. The truth was, for whatever reason, she wanted to be with James.

She looked up at him and shrugged, making the movement carefully casual. "Why not?" Then before he could say anything, she added sternly, "I'm taking your word that it will be strictly business."

"Word of honor," he said, his smile dazzlingly

bright, his relief obvious. "I want only to get back those papers."

"Wait," she said, struck by a sudden thought. "You didn't tell me where we have to go to get the papers. Just how much time are we talking about?"

"Well . . ."

She eyed him suspiciously. "Come on, let's have it. What are you not telling me?"

He grimaced. "The truth is, I have instructions to go to San Jose by . . . *train.*" He said the word as though it were something vulgar.

"Poor James," she said, chuckling at his indignant expression. "By train. How dreadfully bourgeois. Do you think your dignity will survive?"

She sobered somewhat, swallowing her laughter when he directed a squelching stare in her direction.

"The note said I would be contacted if I follow the instructions exactly," he continued. "Which means if you are with me."

She shook her head. "The whole thing sounds pretty fishy to me."

"*Fishy* isn't the word for it," he said dryly. "But it doesn't really matter. I have to get those papers back. And that means if I have to go to San Jose by skateboard, I'll do it."

She laughed at his martyred tone. "You sound like that might be a possibility."

He grinned suddenly, throwing his arm around her as she began to walk again. "If you knew my uncle, you would know that anything's possible. His sense of humor is strange, to say the least."

"Your uncle?"

When they stopped in front of the dressing room door, he leaned against it and gazed down at her, his eyes smiling into hers. "I'll explain all of this tomorrow on the train. Heaven knows we'll have plenty of time for conversation," he added ruefully.

"I'm almost looking forward to it." Her brow creased in thought. "Let's see . . . San Jose. That's about three hundred miles, isn't it?" When he nodded, she said, "Three hundred there, three hundred back." She smiled. "I don't see why we shouldn't be back in plenty of time to make my midnight performance."

She grinned up at him, extending her hand. "Okay, Mr. Halloran, you've got yourself a stooge."

Six

James leaned against a wide column and gazed impatiently around the large, open room of the train station. Every type of person in the world seemed to be in the depot—short, tall, thin, fat—but not one small, cocky woman with bow-shaped lips.

Frowning, he glanced down at his watch. He should have made arrangements to pick her up at her apartment. He should have called her to confirm the time. He should have . . . he should have his head examined for getting involved with her in the first place, he thought with a rueful smile. Where in hell was she?

Slowly he began to examine the people in the room, his gaze making its way toward the wide entrance. He skimmed lightly over a Japanese man carrying an attaché case, a young man in torn jeans, and a woman dressed in a tan trench coat and matching wide-brimmed hat, then moved on.

Suddenly he frowned and retraced his visual route. Something there had struck a chord. The two men had moved on, but the woman was leaning against the wall, a raised newspaper hiding her face. He studied her intently, unable to discover what had caught his eye before.

Then the people in front of the small woman shifted, giving him a clear view, and his lips quivered with laughter as he got a glimpse of pink tights with green polka dots. One small foot was shod in a green high-heeled sandal, the other in a pink one.

As he watched, bemused, he muttered, "She wouldn't. Surely not even Dempsey would . . ."

The newspaper was slowly lowered to reveal bright green heart-shaped sunglasses. Only a few curls of her extravagant mane of hair were visible. The rest were tucked up under the hat, the large brim pulled down like something out of a bad spy movie. After a furtive glance around the room, the newspaper was raised again to hide her face.

James gave a short, low bark of laughter, then maneuvered his way through a group of tourists to get to her side. "For heaven's sake," he said in amused exasperation, "what are you wearing?"

Leaning her head back, she peered up at him from beneath the brim of the extraordinary hat. "What's the matter with what I'm wearing? These are my sleuthing clothes."

"You look like you're working on a remake of *Debbie Does Dallas*," he said dryly as he took her arm and began walking with her across the open space of the terminal. "Couldn't you have worn something less conspicuous?"

She bit her lip, her brow wrinkling as she considered the question. "I don't think I own anything less conspicuous," she said finally.

As they spoke she brushed past a slow-walking, short guru, his somber face belying the humor of his twinkling sky-blue eyes. The various layers of flowing earth-tone fabric contained in his robes and his long gray beard didn't look out of place, but rather seemed a natural part of the technicolored humanity in the terminal.

James glanced back as the man bestowed on them an airy gesture of blessing, then shrugged when he realized the man's costume was no more unconventional than the woman's walking beside him.

"The note said we have to have a private compartment," he said as they got in line to board. "So at least I won't have to watch people staring at you."

She studied his features for a moment. "You're much too inhibited, James," she murmured regretfully. "I'm in a highly visible business. I'm supposed to be stared at."

He didn't like her estimation of his personality. She made him sound very dull, he thought as they walked down the narrow corridor of the train, searching for the right compartment. No one had ever accused him of that before. He was used to words like *dedicated* and *intelligent* being applied to him.

Reaching out, he opened the door and ushered her inside, then said shortly, "So you're used to it. I'm not."

"I've offended you," she said contritely. "I didn't mean to. Really. I wasn't passing judgment, merely making an observation."

Suddenly she laughed and he turned to fix her with a grim stare. "I don't know why I amuse you so much," he said irritably.

She shook her head and bit her lip to stop the laughter. "No, I'm sorry," she said. "It's just that most of the time your expression is totally unreadable, but occasionally what you're thinking comes through loud and clear." She paused, staring up at him with sparkling eyes. "Such as right now."

"And what am I thinking?"

"You're mentally telling me where I can put my observation," she said.

"Very astute of you." He watched in offended silence as she moved around the small compartment, examining each feature as though it were something new and wonderful. Within seconds he had forgotten to be angry with her and was gazing at her in puzzled delight as she exclaimed over the tiny bathroom.

Why did this always happen? he wondered in confusion. She could make him absolutely furious one minute, then the next minute he wanted to catch her in his arms and swing her around in delight.

"And you made fun of my trench coat," she said, breaking into his thoughts. "This place reminds me of an old Hitchcock movie. One of the black-and-whites. Now all we need is to find a dead body in the closet."

"Don't say that," he said, glancing over his shoulder. "The way my luck's been running, we could get one." He motioned to the seat beside him. "Come sit down. We may as well be comfortable while we wait."

Sitting beside him, Dempsey watched the terminal slowly go past and James watched Dempsey, his thoughts centered entirely on her. That first night she had said that they didn't know each other and she was right. He didn't know a thing about this woman. Except that he wanted to make love to her and there was something else. Something he was finding hard to understand. He wanted to protect her, to cherish her. It was an emotion that was new to him, an emotion that perplexed him.

"When did you decide to be a comedienne?" he asked, his voice pensive.

She turned to him and smiled. "Somewhere around the second grade." Her eyes were focusing on the past when she added, "I was chubby and unattractive, but nobody cared about that when I made them laugh." She shook her head as though shaking away the memories. "In high school I was voted Most Witty three years in a row. Not exactly on par with Most Beautiful, but it was *mine*, and no one could take it away."

He frowned, suddenly seeing something beneath the surface that surprised him. "So you just like the attention you get when you make people laugh?"

She shrugged. "That's being too simplistic. Everyone likes to be liked. The attention I receive is part of why I *like* what I do, but it's not why I do it. I do it because it's what I am." She cut her eyes up at him. "What are you anyway, a closet shrink?"

"You intrigue me," he said, trying to explain to her what he couldn't explain to himself. "What you say shows that you have a basic insecurity and instead of withdrawing inside yourself, you compensate by calling attention to yourself constantly. It's very interesting."

Giving a choking laugh, she said, "Thank you, Dr. Freud. You've just saved me years of analysis and thousands of dollars. Actually," she added with a grin, "I was looking forward to the day that I could afford to be fashionably mentally disturbed and bore a psychoanalyst to tears with my neuroses."

He laughed, his eyes trained on her face as she swept the hat from her head. Her hair was pushed up and pinned in the back, curls drooping seductively onto her brow. Reaching out, he began to play with a strand. "Didn't you have any other interests in school? Poetry or science?"

"Let's just say I wasn't academically inclined," she said ruefully, then, shrugging out of the coat, she added, "I was on the basketball team in high school. Does that count?"

He examined her skeptically, his eyes measuring the diminutive form encased in a green striped sundress. "You're kidding, of course."

"No, honest." She shook her head. "I was a pretty good guard, but I decided to quit after a couple of weeks."

"Oh?"

"Yeah, I kept getting my face shoved into various and assorted bosoms and decided it just wasn't my game," she said wryly.

He leaned just a fraction of an inch closer, inhaling the scent of her that unexplainably seemed so familiar to him. "So then what did you do?" he murmured.

Dempsey glanced up, her eyes meeting his hesitantly. She hadn't realized he was so close. She could feel his breath on her forehead and shivered uncontrollably. She swallowed heavily, but her voice was still husky when she said, "I gave up sports for country and western music."

"What a switch," he said slowly.

The words were right. It sounded like an ordinary, pleasant conversation, but the conversation between their bodies was anything but ordinary and the sensation attacking her nervous system went far beyond pleasant.

She gave a halting little laugh. "Some friends of mine had a group called the Good Ole Boys and I—I played tambourine with them for a while. They said they needed a little color," she added, exhaling slowly as she felt him touch her hair again.

"Did you enjoy it?"

Enjoy it? she thought wildly. Enjoy what? What were they talking about? Was he conscious of what he was doing to her? Somehow she didn't think so and that made it worse. This wasn't a deliberate attempt to excite her. She wasn't even sure he knew that he was touching her.

With difficulty she raised her eyes to his face. He was staring at the wall across the room. As though feeling her eyes on him, he glanced down at her to give her a questioning look.

"What was the question again?" she said faintly.

"Did you enjoy playing with the country and western band?" he said, and a smile of unconscious sensuality curved his strong lips.

"Actually, I performed with them only one time," she admitted. "When they started singing 'She took my heart and stomped that sucker flat,' I decided they had all the color they needed."

He laughed, leaning back on the couch, and Dempsey inhaled in relief when he reluctantly released the lock of hair he had been fondling.

James shifted in his seat, feeling awkward. He suddenly wished he smoked so that he would have something to do with his hands. They had an alarming tendency to touch her without his permission.

Frowning, he inhaled and said, "Didn't your parents encourage you in anything else, or did they want you to be a comedienne?"

She remained silent for a moment, gazing out the window at the passing scenery. She was smiling, but the hands that rested in her lap were clenched into fists. At last she relaxed visibly and turned to smile up at him. "Turnabout's fair play. What about you? Were you a sober-headed whiz kid when you were young?"

"When I was young?" He frowned, giving her an offended look. "When I was a *child*," he corrected her, "I suppose I was just a regular kid. In fact, Johnny reminds me a lot of myself. Always getting into trouble but never maliciously."

"What happened?" When he gave her a questioning look she added, "To change you into Mr. I'll-stand-for-no-nonsense Executive?"

When his expression changed, Dempsey ducked her head, scratching her nose to hide a grin. Now he was definitely annoyed.

"I grew up," he said shortly. "Most people do." He glanced at her. "At least most normal people do."

"How dull," she murmured, then shrugged. "You look like a very efficient man. How come you're chasing all over the country like this, meeting men in dark alleys and getting mysterious notes?"

"Uncle Charlie," he said in resignation.

"Uncle Charlie?"

"My Uncle Charlie of the handcuffs. He decided that I was too wrapped up in my work." He shook his head. "That's all right. His concern I can handle. But to combat my absorption he took some valuable papers from my desk. Papers that don't belong to me. How in hell he thinks this farce is going to straighten out my life, I don't know. But he sent me to that alley and now he's sending me on this wild-goose chase to keep me from losing my job. It just doesn't make sense."

She laughed. "He sounds like fun. I really think I would like your Uncle Charlie."

"You would," he agreed dryly, then he frowned. "I'm worried about him. He was a detective with the LAPD for over thirty years." He smiled. "Disguises were his specialty. I don't know, maybe retirement has left him with too much time on his hands. It has to be hard for a man as active as Uncle Charlie to accept that he's no longer needed." He shrugged restlessly. "I think if Aunt Carey were still alive, this wouldn't be happening, but without his job, without his wife, Irene and I are all he has. Still, none of that explains why he's suddenly gone berserk. He's always enjoyed playing practical jokes, but never anything like this. This could get him into real trouble."

"Wait," she protested. "I don't think you're being fair. You think he's crazy just because he wants a better life for you?"

"Better according to his standards," he said grimly. "I'm a grown man. Surely I have the right to choose my own life-style."

Slipping out of her shoes, she folded her legs up on the seat beside her while she carefully considered the problem. "What kind of relationship do you have with your uncle?" she asked finally.

"We've always been close. Why?"

"Then he knows you." She turned sideways to gaze at him earnestly. "He obviously sees something in your life that you've overlooked, some change for the worse. Isn't he doing it out of love?"

He shook his head. "I see what you're getting at, but that doesn't make it any less illegal. And there is a possibility that he could go to jail for this."

She shrugged off his suggestion. "He's an ex-cop. He knows the consequences. He's obviously willing to be humiliated in front of men who were his colleagues just to straighten you out. That sounds like a nice man who's willing to go to bat for people he loves."

James frowned at her. He didn't want to talk about

Uncle Charlie. He didn't want to admit what she was saying might be true. Standing abruptly, he said, "Come on, let's scare up some lunch."

She followed meekly behind him as he walked down the hall toward the dining car. Because of the early hour, the car was only half full when they took their seats. After ordering, Dempsey looked around at the other diners.

A short, dapper priest with a shock of white hair who was seated at the table behind James caught her eye and she smiled at him, then continued her examination of the room.

"See that couple over there," she whispered to James, moving her head slightly to the right.

He turned, taking a moment to study the middle-aged couple, then looked back at Dempsey. "What about them?"

"What do you figure they are to each other? Husband and wife? Brother and sister? Lovers?" she added slyly.

"How should I know? I've never seen them before in my life."

She sent him a pitying glance. "Don't you have an imagination? Look at her dress. It's not exactly Dior, but it's brand new. And that red scarf is a dead giveaway."

"I don't know what you're talking about."

"She's definitely out to get someone. I'll bet that man with her is not related to her." She tilted her head, considering the problem. "He's—he's her employer," she said finally. "But she wants to make the relationship something more personal."

A smile spread across his lips as he felt her enthusiasm. "And what makes you think that?"

"The expression on her face. She's wishing he would notice her instead of reading that book."

Suddenly the couple stood and walked past Dempsey and James on their way out.

"Oh, and Martha," the man said as they walked. "Don't forget to remind me to call the insurance company tomorrow. They haven't sent those forms yet."

"Yes, Mr. Newbolt," the woman said quietly.

Dempsey turned back to James with a triumphant laugh. "What did I tell you?"

"How did you know he was her boss?" he asked suspiciously.

"I'm brilliant, that's how," she said smugly. "I've been a student of human nature all my life." She waved her hand airily. "I get certain vibes."

"Vibes, my foot," he said, his tone blatantly disbelieving.

She grinned suddenly. "Her steno pad was sticking out of her purse and he was reading a book on corporate structure . . . but there were vibes, too."

"Okay," he said, looking around the room. "What do your vibes tell you about those two men in the corner?"

She turned to study the two in question. A scant second later she glanced back at James. "Too easy. They're not related . . . nor are they lovers," she added cheekily. "They're business associates."

Gazing at her in bewilderment, he glanced at the men, then back to her. "How can you know that without even looking for clues?"

She shrugged. "Their clues are on their faces. They smile exactly like you and Charis do."

"Chloe," he said, frowning. "That sounds like an insult. Would you care to explain what you mean?"

"Watch the eyes," she said, nodding toward the men. "When they smile, there are lines here." She demonstrated by smiling, pointing to the lines around her mouth. "Now turn around and watch the priest behind you smile."

When James swung around in his seat, Dempsey glanced at the priest and smiled, expecting and getting a warm smile in return.

James turned slowly in his seat, a pensive expression on his face.

"You see," she said. "There were lines here and here." She indicated her forehead and eyes.

"I don't think I want to hear any more about the business associates," he said ruefully.

"Okay," she said agreeably. "What about that couple across the aisle?"

"Let me guess this time," he said as he studied the attractive couple. After a moment he said, "They're newlyweds. They can't keep their eyes—or their hands—off each other."

"Wrong," she replied at once.

"What do you mean wrong?" he said indignantly. "This is all speculation. They could very well be newly married." He eyed her smile sourly. "Okay, so what are they?"

"They are illicit lovers," she said, leaning forward to whisper across the table. "They're getting away for a night alone."

"Okay, that tears it," he said, throwing down his napkin. "There is no way you could know that. What's your evidence?"

She favored him with a superior smile. "Elementary, Watson. She's not wearing a wedding ring."

"That doesn't mean anything. Not all women wear them."

"But he is," Dempsey continued placidly. "And he keeps looking over his shoulder as though he's afraid of seeing someone he knows. Now do you concede?"

"No," he said stubbornly, then when she continued to stare at him, he said, "I'll concede the bulk of the evidence is in your favor."

"Big of you. Mighty big of you." She caught his eye and they both began to laugh, unaware that they were the object of more than one person's speculation.

As soon as they had finished their meal they left the dining car, followed closely by a priest with white hair and twinkling blue eyes.

They had not been in their compartment for five minutes when a porter knocked on the door, handing James a sealed white envelope.

"Another one," Dempsey said, her eyes sparkling with excitement. "I wonder if your uncle gave it to the porter in LA or if he's on the train. I'd like to meet him."

"He'd be hard to find, believe me," James said. "When he puts on one of his disguises, even I can't spot him."

"Disguises? How exciting!" Suddenly her eyes widened. "Of course, the old broad. That was him too."

James nodded, then sat down on the couch to open

the envelope, with Dempsey sitting close beside him. He read it carefully, then handed it to her.

In the city of old San Jose,
You'll find many a sought-after pleasure.
But the Laundromat on Fifth Street
Holds the key to your counterfeit treasure.

"His poetry is getting better," she murmured. Then she glanced up at James, a comical look on her small face. "A Laundromat?"

He nodded in resignation. "A Laundromat."

Seven

Little more than an hour later James paid off the cab that had brought them to a small, unspectacular Laundromat on Fifth Street.

"Why couldn't your uncle send us to someplace glamorous?" Dempsey asked as she stared at the tan brick building. "I wouldn't mind searching a nice French restaurant . . . but a Laundromat?"

The interior was no more glamorous than the exterior. An attempt had been made some years earlier to brighten the room, but time had faded the pink walls to shades of dirty beige. A large woman stood at one of the turquoise washing machines, hauling wet clothes into a wire basket. Two more talked in quiet voices as they folded towels and sheets, while a young father with two children in tow fed change into a drink machine. The children were the only ones who seemed to notice the new arrivals.

Dempsey glanced up at James. "You know, since I've known you, I've encountered a larger variety of smells than I have in the whole of the rest of my life." She sniffed delicately. "Laundromats should smell clean, but they always end up smelling like a locker at the Y."

"Do you have some kind of nose obsession? We're not here to smell." He glanced quickly around the small room. "We're here to find those papers."

When he began searching the cracks between the washing machines, Dempsey shrugged and stuck her head inside the first dryer. She had just opened the door to the third when the large woman jerked the door out of Dempsey's hand and began to throw her clothes inside.

"Wait a minute," Dempsey said with indignant surprise. "My head was in this dryer before your sheets."

"Dryers are for drying clothes," the woman said, hands on hips. "I don't know what you were doing to it, but my clothes are in it now and they're going to stay there."

She raised her chin to stare haughtily at the older woman. "That's perfectly ridiculous. There's a whole roomful of dryers. Why steal mine?"

The woman stepped closer, looking down at Dempsey from what seemed like an extraordinary height. "Where's it say your name on it?"

Dempsey's eyes blazed with outrage and she moved

a step forward, refusing to back down. Her eyes narrowed as she began in a low voice, "Why, you—"

"Dempsey!" James grabbed her arm, quickly jerking her away from the dryer. "Can't you stay out of trouble for five minutes?"

"But she stole my dryer!" she said, glaring at the rude woman over her shoulder. "I can't let her get away with that."

He leaned down to whisper in her ear. "The woman weighs at least two hundred pounds. She would massacre you."

"Oh, yeah?" she said, but some of the belligerence went out of her voice as the truth of what he said sunk in. "Well—well, it's just lucky for her that I don't have time to tangle with her. I know a few tricks that would put her away."

She glanced up and saw the laughter in his eyes. "You're right," she admitted ruefully. "She would take my tricks and sit on them. The woman has more hair on her arms than my agent has on his chest," she muttered as she glanced around for a new place to search. "Where would I be if I were a secret document?" Her eyes opened wide. "I've got it, James."

Beckoning, she guided him to the soap machine on the far wall. "This is it," she said, her voice positive. "I'm sure of it. The papers will be taped behind this machine. Pull it away from the wall."

He looked at her, then at the heavy machine. "You've got to be kidding."

"Trust me," she said bracingly. "It was simply a matter of logical deduction."

After five minutes of strenuous exertion, the soap

machine was away from the wall and James was against it, breathing heavily as he stared at Dempsey with vengeance in his eyes. "Logical deduction, right? You want to know what I think of your logic?"

She didn't, of course. With a smile and a shrug she said, "Is it my fault that your uncle doesn't have a logical mind?"

Her brow creased in thought, she walked to one of the folding tables and hopped up, swinging her legs idly as she concentrated on the problem. Placing her hands on the edge, she leaned forward to eye him in curiosity. "You certainly do get yourself into strange situations, James."

He muttered something that sounded like an incantation under his breath and walked toward her slowly, but before he could carry out his obvious intention to strangle her, a look of surprise crossed her face. She leaned farther forward, groping for something on the underside of the table. Suddenly she jumped down and fell to her knees beside it.

"James," she squealed in breathless excitement. "I think this is it."

Kneeling beside her, he peered under the table. Taped to the underside was a small white envelope.

"That's why I couldn't find it," she said. "It's another dumb poem. Dumb poems would naturally not hang around in the same places as secret documents." She nodded. "Depend on it, if it had been a secret document, it would have been behind the soap machine."

His eyes lit with amusement, but he said, "Will you shut up for a minute so that I can read it?"

She looked over his shoulder and read out loud:

The blessings of Ra shine on all
And they are within your reach.
If exposing all is what you want,
Take a bus to Stratford-on-the-Beach.
Reposing on the clubhouse lawn,
Venus reigns in all her glory,
Search her beauty well and you will find
A key to your circumambulatory.

"*Circumambulatory?* That's not a word," she said in disgust. "If that's what you call poetic license, someone ought to revoke his license." She glanced up at James. "What do Ra and Venus have to do with anything? And where on earth is Stratford-on-the-Beach? Because if it's not in the contiguous United States, you can forget it."

"Hush," he said, chuckling. "People are staring."

"And well they should. We're chasing all over California to read bad poetry when I wouldn't go out of town for the *good* stuff."

He took her arm and pulled her out of the building. On the street he glanced down at her. "I've never heard of this Stratford-on-the-Beach. It sounds like one of those cutesy developments that have everything but good taste and cost a fortune to buy into."

"I would say it's probably near the ocean," she offered helpfully.

"Your perspicacity is awe-inspiring," he said, then exhaled noisily. "I guess we go to the bus station and

find out where this Shangri-la is, then buy tickets."
He shook his head. "Sometimes he amazes me."

"He?"

"Uncle Charlie. He said that I don't interact with
people enough. This bus trip is obviously his way of
forcing contact on me."

She glanced up at him curiously. "Haven't you ever
ridden a bus?"

He raised a hand to hail a passing cab, then lowered it when it passed him by. "Certainly I have. Lots
of times."

Her eyes narrowed in suspicion. "When?"

Staring down at her with aloof dignity, he asked,
"What do you mean when? Am I supposed to give specific dates?"

"Yeah, that would be good," she said, unaffected by
his haughty posture. "Give me specific dates." When
he held his silence she began to laugh. "Oh, James,
you poor thing. You can't fool me. If you ever rode a
bus, it was to and from grade school."

His stiff features softened at the sound of her
laughter, and he reached out to pull her into his
arms. "You're a devil." He kissed the tip of her nose.
"But I am not a 'poor James.' You make me sound
underprivileged because I don't have to ride a hot,
crowded bus."

"You are," she said, smiling up at him. "The most
interesting people in the world ride buses. In fact, I
would say I have made more friends on buses than on
any other mode of transportation."

"How often do you ride submarines?" he asked,
then shrugged. "All right, I'll reserve judgment until

after this trip is over." He raised his hand again when he saw a taxi on their side of the street. "Right now I simply want to get to the bus station."

"Just one small question?" she asked in a small voice.

"What?"

"I hate to mention it, but the note didn't say if we take a local bus or a cross-country."

When the cab stopped, he helped her inside, then spoke to the driver. He turned to her as soon as he was seated beside her. "The driver says it's not local, so that answers one question."

The others were answered as soon as they arrived at the bus station. Stratford-on-the-Beach was approximately sixty-three miles from San Jose and they would have to wait only five minutes for a departing bus, giving James just enough time to call his office.

"Did you remember to make those reservations? No, turn that over to Peterson. He can take care of it, but reschedule my appointment with Lyell for Monday. I want to handle him myself."

Dempsey watched James's face as he spoke. He had unconsciously slipped back into his sober business personality. The change was fascinating. Minutes before he had been teasing and laughing with her. Now it was as though nothing existed except his work.

After he replaced the receiver, it was several minutes before the executive disappeared and her partner in adventure reasserted himself.

The sleek, modern bus was almost full when James

and Dempsey stepped into it, but they managed to find two seats together near the back.

James glanced around skeptically, his eyes passing a stout woman with blond curls and twinkling sky-blue eyes, to settle on a young, scruffy man who slept with his mouth open.

Leaning close to Dempsey, he said, "I suppose he's one of the interesting people you were telling me about." He nodded slowly. "Yes, I can certainly see your point."

She giggled, then before he could stop her, leaned forward to tap the man who sat in front of them on the shoulder. "Excuse me. We'd like to introduce ourselves. I'm Dempsey Turner-Riley and this is James Halloran."

"Glad to meet you, Dempsey. James," the older man said. "I'm Frank Finneman, and this is my wife, Louise."

Dempsey leaned her head to the side, listening. "That's not a California accent. I would guess Pennsylvania."

"That's right," Louise said in pleased surprise. "We're on the last leg of a cross-country tour. Our daughter lives about two hundred miles south of here."

"How interesting," James said under his breath, then grinned when Dempsey poked him in the ribs.

"I take it you're both retired."

Frank laughed. "The gray hair must be a give-away," he said. "Well, you know what they say about old soldiers."

"No," Dempsey said, leaning closer. "What do they say?"

" 'Old soldiers never die; they just fade away.' "

She glanced at the woman beside him. "And do their wives fade away too?"

"Actually I was a schoolteacher. Frank and I arranged it so that we could retire at the same time."

Two young men across the aisle had been listening openly to the conversation. They both looked over twenty-one, but they were young enough to grimace and roll their eyes at the mention of schoolteachers.

Dempsey hid her smile at their expressions and glanced back to Louise. "I guess you could say old schoolteachers just 'grade' away."

James looked pained. "You could, but I wish you hadn't," he muttered.

The young men laughed and the one by the window leaned across his friend to say, "Cecil's on the swim team. He would probably just wade away."

Everyone around them was laughing now. From behind them a voice said proudly, "I'm a used car salesman."

Dempsey turned to the neat, well-built man. Her brow creased in thought for a moment. "Old used car salesmen never die . . ." she said slowly, then shrugged. "They just move to Pomona."

The man joined the others in laughter as Dempsey turned to James. "Old executives never die—" she began.

"They reach a compromise," he finished dryly.

"Why, James," she said in pleased surprise. "You made a joke."

"You don't have to sound so astonished. I have a sense of humor."

"Yes," she agreed doubtfully. "But somehow your dignity keeps tripping it up."

In an astonishingly short time Dempsey knew the life story of every person who sat close enough to them to question. James was amazed at the way people responded to her enthusiasm. When she fell asleep in the seat beside him, he stared down at her, his face sober.

She looked like a baby in her sleep. A sweet, tender-lipped baby, he thought. She looked so vulnerable, he wanted to hold her fast and protect her from harm. Not that she made him feel in any way fatherly, he admitted silently. The truth was far from it and there was the danger . . . He had told her the night before that the trip would be strictly business. And he had meant it then, but good intentions and a dollar would get you a cup of coffee. He was having an extremely difficult time thinking of her in anything other than a very personal, very intimate way.

He had the feeling that she would allow the relationship to develop on more intimate lines if he were a different kind of man, and the notion irritated him. He knew they were different, had different life-styles, but there was a basic attraction that couldn't be denied. Why, James wondered, should a man from her own crowd—a man who couldn't possibly want her as much as he himself did—be able to touch her, hold her when he wasn't allowed to?

Suddenly his stomach muscles constricted at the thought of an unknown man making love to her. His eyes narrowed in unexplainable anger, then he frowned. What in hell was she doing to him? he questioned himself in exasperation.

Leaning back in the seat, he felt as if he were on a merry-go-round. One minute he felt like strangling her, then she would do something that would totally captivate him.

He would have to resolve this thing with Dempsey before he could go ahead with Chloe. It wouldn't be fair to Chloe. It was odd that he had never considered before what was fair to Chloe. Why was he suddenly so aware of other people and their feelings? It wasn't a comfortable sensation.

He shook his head. He was just tired, he decided. When he got back to his apartment, got back to his life, things would continue as they always had. He frowned. Suddenly that thought didn't give him any pleasure. Everything had changed.

James brooded silently as bits of California passed by the window. When the bus neared their destination, he glanced down at Dempsey and his confusion was forgotten.

Leaning down, he curved his fingers around her cheek and chin. Her skin felt warm and as soft as kidskin. "Dempsey," he murmured. "Sweetheart, we're almost there."

When she sighed in her sleep and curved her body toward him, he felt a muscle-clenching heat rise from the center of him. She was more sensual unconsciously than most of the women he knew were consciously. And maybe that was why she was so appealing, he thought. Because it was unstudied, completely natural.

"Dempsey," he said louder, then caught his breath when her eyes opened and met his, a lazy smile curving her soft lips.

"Hello," she said, her voice husky with sleep. "Are we there?"

He nodded, unable to speak when her lips were so near. Clearing his throat, he leaned back. "Any minute now. You'd better get your shoes on."

They created a minor stir as they searched for the pink shoe, which had somehow become separated from the green one, which could have accounted for the peculiar look the bus driver gave them as he drove away. But in any case they were soon standing on the side of the road before a rustic wooden entrance and an enormous, brightly painted billboard, its message confirming they had reached their destination.

Dempsey waved to the retreating bus, then turned to stare at the entrance of the resort. She glanced up at James. "A guard," she said, nodding toward the small structure that divided the street.

"Yes, I noticed," he said unemotionally. "It can't be helped. We'll just have to convince him that we have friends who live here."

But after five minutes with the pleasantly stubborn old man who guarded the entrance, they knew it wouldn't be so easy.

". . . but my Cousin Molly is so absentminded," Dempsey said earnestly, gazing up at the guard as he peered out of the window at them. "She probably forgot to tell you that we were visiting her today."

"If you could tell me her name, miss," he said helpfully. "I could phone her and confirm it."

"What *is* her last name?" Dempsey said, a finger on her cheek as she tilted her head to the side. "She married that awful man with the tattoo. My memory is so bad," she added, shaking her head.

"It runs in the family," James muttered.

She opened her eyes wide. "Oh, I know, it was something that began with an *N*."

"I'm sorry, miss," he said firmly, his eyes clouding with suspicion. "I can't give out the names of the residents. You'll either have to give me a name or move along."

When it became clear the man would not change his mind and in fact was considering taking steps to have them removed, James pulled Dempsey a few yards away from the entrance. He turned to stare at the high wooden fence that surrounded the exclusive grounds. "Damn Uncle Charlie," he said. "This was all for nothing. I should have known at the beginning."

"You don't mean you're going to let a little bitty fence stop you," she said in disbelief. "How can you give up now?"

"Easy," he said. "I call a cab."

"James," she said, putting her hand through his arm and walking away from the entrance parallel to the fence. "Faint heart never kept anyone out of jail."

He winced at her bluntness. "Okay, I see your point. But what can we do? That little bitty fence is seven feet high."

"We'll just have to use our ingenuity."

"We'll just have to use our ingenuity," he mimicked as she laughed up at him. "Sometimes your ingenuity scares the hell out of me."

Glancing around, James spotted a metal garbage can and hauled it over to the wooden fence. After carefully surveying the other side for possible hazards, he pulled himself over, then called for Dempsey to follow.

She stood on the can and peered over the fence. James was directly below her. "Hurry up," he whispered, "before someone comes out of one of the houses and catches us."

"It sure is a long way down," she said warily.

"Just jump, for heaven's sake. I'll catch you."

She stared at him for a second. "Did you read that interesting study about trust between husbands and wives? They made them turn their backs to their spouses and then simply fall backwards. Do you know how many couldn't do that because they didn't trust enough?"

"No," he said in frustration. "I don't. I also don't know why you're bringing it up now."

"Well, I don't know either," she said, habitually honest. "But it was a lot of them. And if people who have been married for years and years can't trust each other, why should I trust a man I've known for only a week?"

"*Jump,*" he ordered.

With her hands she hauled herself up on top of the fence. Then, closing her eyes, she jumped . . . and landed in his arms with a soft *whoosh* of escaping breath. Opening her eyes, she gazed up at him and smiled. "I guess none of them were married to you."

He didn't smile in response. His eyes were focused on her mouth, and without warning he tightened his hands on her waist, bringing her forcefully closer as he leaned down to bring his lips to hers.

She moaned faintly, receiving him hungrily. Pushing her hands between them, she moved them up to his neck, clasping it to hold him there.

They were both breathing heavily when the kiss ended sometime later. James ran an unsteady hand through his hair and drew in a deep breath. "Now," he said as though nothing had happened. "To find the clubhouse."

Her eyes were dazed as she followed meekly behind him. Luckily it wasn't a large community, and the clubhouse was relatively easy to find.

"It's odd that we haven't seen any people on the streets," he said as they pushed through the shrubbery that surrounded the clubhouse grounds. "We've seen them in cars, coming in and leaving. But no children playing in the streets."

"It's probably a retirement community," she murmured, parting two branches to peek through. "They probably don't allow anyone under fifty. Wait, I think I see the statue of Venus. It—" She broke off suddenly, a gasp escaping her as she viewed the members of the resort enjoying the facilities of the clubhouse. "Oh, James," she whispered, laughter bubbling up in her voice.

"What is it?" He moved from behind her to peer through the branches. "What's so damn fun—" His sentence was cut off in mid-word as he discovered just exactly what she had seen. "It's a damned—"

"It's a nudist colony!" she finished for him. "What fun! Ra," she said suddenly, snapping her fingers. "The Egyptian sun god." She smothered her laughter in his shoulder, then looked up at him. "He was giving us clues. Remember the note said, 'If exposing all is what you want.' " She gestured toward the clubhouse. "You can't get more exposed than that. Very ingenious."

"I'm glad you appreciate it," he said. "But what in hell are we going to do now? We'll never get in there without being noticed."

She slowly lifted eyes shining with mischief. "I guess we'll have to expose all."

"You're kidding," he said in disbelief. "You expect me to—to—"

"To bare all," she said, then shrugged. "He's your uncle, and those are your secret papers in there on Venus."

Frowning, he stared down at her, then looked again at the people who were engaged in various sports on the other side of the shrubbery. Suddenly his eyes narrowed. "Wait a minute. Look at those people coming out of that door." He indicated a side entrance. "They all have towels wrapped around them. At least for a little while," he added when the thin woman he had been watching dropped her towel in a hamper.

"It's probably the sauna," Dempsey said. "We get into our towels and simply walk through it on our way outside."

"Well, don't just stand there," he said irritably. "Let's get it over with."

Fifteen minutes later Dempsey stepped out the same door they had spotted earlier and glanced around to find James. He was leaning against the wall, looking very casual and at home, but she grinned when she realized he was having a problem finding something to do with his hands.

Walking up to him, she whispered, "You never appreciate pockets until you lose them."

"Dempsey," he said urgently, grabbing her arm. "Let's find that damn statue. I feel like a fool."

That was not how he looked. She hadn't realized how muscular he was. Dark hair spread across his chest, narrowing on its path to his hard, flat stomach. The white towel looked vaguely barbaric and lent a basic sensuality to his lean good looks.

He raised a brow when he caught her studying him and unbelievably, she blushed. "I think I could get used to this place," she quipped.

His eyes traveled over her figure, exploring every inch of bare flesh. "Not me," he murmured. "I'm afraid my mind runs in channels too basic for comfort. I would never get anything done with you around."

A middle-aged man walked by them, his steps slowing as he eyed Dempsey's towel. "Chest cold," she explained blithely, pointing to her chest. "My doctor said I should keep it out of drafts."

When the man passed by, James laughed. "Are you never at a loss?" Suddenly his eyes narrowed. "There's our Venus," he said, nodding to the right.

When he began to walk toward it, Dempsey noticed a woman staring after him. She had dropped out of a volleyball game when James passed her, and Dempsey studied her closely. She was young, blond, very attractive—and quite obviously interested in James rather than the oddity of his towel.

When the woman began to walk toward James, Dempsey caught up with her quickly. "I wouldn't bother," she murmured to the blond woman who glanced at her in inquiry. "An old war injury," she continued, nodding toward James's towel. "That's why I talked him into coming here. He's still self-conscious about his handicap and I thought it would help to get everything out in the open, so to speak."

The woman gave James a startled look, her eyes dropping to the towel, then back to Dempsey. "You mean . . . ?"

Dempsey nodded significantly. "Remember Jake Barnes in *The Sun Also Rises*?" She shook her head in regret, sighing as she glanced at James. "Same thing . . . only worse," she added for good measure.

Smiling smugly, she watched the woman return to the game, then suddenly found James standing beside her. "What are you doing? I thought you were right behind me." He gave her a suspicious, narrow-eyed look. "What were you saying to that woman?"

Dempsey shrugged and smiled. "She wanted to know what color nail polish I use."

He gazed down at her for a moment. "Then why was she staring at me?"

"Was she staring at you?" She glanced at the statue that stood in the middle of the grounds. "You really should stop fooling around, James. We need to find those papers."

"You—" he sputtered helplessly as she walked away from him.

By the time James reached her she was triumphantly pulling a small envelope from the marigolds that surrounded the base of the statue.

After returning to the clubhouse, they slipped into their clothes and, while the guard was busy checking someone coming in, they were busy slipping out.

Eight

Obtain a private compartment
On the Sacramento express.
Then you will be so very near
The thing that you want best.

James laid the note on the seat between them and stared out the taxi window. "I'm getting sick of this," he said tightly. "It's all been for nothing." He paused. "But I can't believe Uncle Charlie put me through this for nothing. He simply wants me to suffer before he gives me the papers. They simply have to be in Sacramento."

"I can't go."

He swung his head around to her. "What did you say?"

"I can't go," she repeated. "If I don't start for home right now, I won't make the midnight show."

He picked up her hand. "But you can't desert me now. Somehow I feel that you're the key. I don't know why it should be that way." He shook his head in confusion. "I don't know what in hell's in the old fool's mind, but he insisted in the first note that you be with me. If you're not, I'll never get those papers back."

She leaned her head against the window, staring at the passing scenery. It made her sad to think that their adventure was over. And she wanted to help him—she really did—but she couldn't forget her obligations. She had a career that demanded single-minded dedication. She couldn't let what she had built up slip through her fingers.

She raised her eyes. "I'm sorry," she began, then suddenly she was caught by the look in his eyes. She felt like Alice—only the rabbit hole into which she sank was warm and velvet-lined and overpoweringly irresistible.

As their eyes held, the Green Duck and the midnight show faded into oblivion. She suddenly found it difficult to remember why she had been so concerned. Nothing mattered except the way she felt when he stared at her with that pleading, vulnerable look in his eyes.

"Dempsey?" he prompted softly.

"Well," she said huskily, "I guess it wouldn't hurt to

miss one show. I'll call Mr. Petrov—the manager—when we get to the station."

Laughing in triumph, he pulled her into his arms to squeeze her tightly. "You won't regret it," he assured her. "We can't give up when we're so close."

The words were a husky whisper against her forehead that sent shivers of desire up her spine. He tilted her chin to deliver a soft, swimmingly sweet kiss. "And like you said, it won't hurt to miss just one show."

Mr. Petrov, however, didn't share this opinion. To say he was not pleased was an understatement, and Dempsey bit her lip as she hung up the phone in the terminal. She only hoped she wasn't burning any bridges. Even jobs like the one at the Green Duck were difficult to come by.

"I'd better check in with the office while we're here," James said, his voice distracted as he glanced at his watch. He had taken care of their tickets while Dempsey talked to Mr. Petrov. "And I need to call Chloe. We had a dinner date tonight," he added as he picked up one of the receivers.

Once again the sober businessman took over as he questioned his secretary about office events. And oddly, when he called the blond woman Dempsey had met earlier in the week, his face didn't change from the executive mode.

In a couple of minutes he hung up, frowning slightly. Dempsey walked silently beside him as he began to make his way toward the train.

"Well, how's Cloris?" she asked. "Is she mad because you broke your date?"

"Chloe," he corrected her automatically. "No, she wasn't angry." His frown deepened. "In fact, she was very understanding."

He spoke in a slow monotone, as though he were turning over a problem in his mind. His features were reflective as Dempsey studied him, and she wondered again about his relationship with the blond woman.

"She's nice," Dempsey offered conversationally. "I like her."

"Yes, she's nice," he murmured.

"Too nice," she said meaningfully.

He stopped walking to give her a questioning glance. "Why do you say 'too nice' in that portentous way? You sound as though you're accusing me of something."

"I mean she's too nice for you. She seems like a very sincere sort of person. While you, I'm afraid, are not a sincere person, James," she said slowly, her expression indicating regret. She glanced sideways at him. "She deserves someone better than you."

"Thank you very much," he said, his features tightening. Where in hell did she get off making a statement like that? he fumed silently. What did she know about his life, his character? She was just—

He stopped his thoughts abruptly. She knew a lot more than he wanted her to, he admitted ruefully. He had planned on using Chloe, thoughtlessly using another human being for his own purposes. He deserved Dempsey's criticism.

But that was before, he thought in surprise. Something had changed since then. He didn't know how or why, but he could no longer dispassionately think of marrying to have children and normalize his life.

Without understanding the reason, he knew he wanted Dempsey to know of the change. He turned to her to explain how he felt and found her staring at a newsstand, a strange, troubled look on her expressive features.

"What is it?" he asked in concern.

She didn't move or take her eyes off the newspapers. "What's today?" she said quietly.

"Today? It's Thursday, the twenty-second."

"The twenty-second," she repeated dully, her eyes vague. Then she inhaled deeply and glanced up at him, smiling in a way that made him want to take her in his arms to comfort her. "I guess I'd better call," she said so reluctantly that he hurt for her.

Walking back to the line of pay phones, she picked up the receiver of one and quietly arranged with the operator to make a collect call from Eleanor to a town called Blue Lake in northern California.

"Mama?" she said hesitantly. "How are you?"

She was silent for a few minutes, listening with her eyes closed, a pained expression on her small face. James could hear the faint sound of a woman talking.

"Yes—yes, I know. I'll try to phone you more often, but"—she forced a smile as she talked—"you know how show business is; I don't have much time for anything. No, Mama, of course it's not more important than you." She sighed shakily. "I just wanted to wish you a happy birthday. Did you get lots of presents?"

The smile slipped into a strained silence again as she listened. James couldn't believe what he was seeing. This was nothing like the Dempsey he knew, fearless, audacious, always laughing. The unhappiness in her eyes was wrong, absolutely wrong.

After a while she said, "Mama, did you talk to Dr. Ragsdale about this? No—no, please, calm down, Mama. I'm sure you're right, but I thought he was helping you. Who are you seeing now?" She inhaled shakily. "Maybe if you wouldn't think about the bad things all the time—

"I try to understand," she said after a moment. "I just thought if maybe you get out of the house more, maybe you could meet new people and—

"Yes, I guess you know what's best for you. I was just trying to help."

She leaned against the wall, her eyes closed, her pale face tightly under control. She listened in silence for almost ten minutes before she spoke again.

"Mama—*Mama*," she repeated louder, then inhaled and said quietly, "Mama, I love you."

For a moment there was a vulnerable, expectant look on her face, then she swallowed roughly and James could hear a shrill voice talking quickly on the other end.

Then with surprising abruptness Dempsey said, "I've got to go. I promise I'll call again soon. 'Bye, Mama," she said quickly, and replaced the receiver, looking at once relieved and disappointed.

After a moment she glanced up at James. "Mothers," she said, a bright forced smile curving her soft lips as she shook her head ruefully. "They're the major cause of gray hair."

She looked around the station as though coming out of a daze. "Hadn't we better start moving? We don't want to miss our train."

"Dempsey—" he began.

"I'm starving," she said, interrupting him with feverish enthusiasm. Grabbing his hand, she began to pull him toward the train. "Let's find the dining car again. The food at lunch wasn't half bad." She grinned. "Who am I trying to kid? After all that peanut butter, it was wonderful."

All through dinner she kept up the lively, inconsequential chatter and James found it a painful experience. It hurt to see her trying so hard to be funny.

On returning to their compartment they found that the bed had been made and Dempsey began to flit around the small space like an unhappy butterfly.

"Dempsey," he said, catching her by the hand.

"Yes?" she said, smiling determinedly.

He pulled her down to sit beside him on the bed. "Let's talk."

"Sure," she said amiably. "We could talk about politics, religion . . . the weather?"

"We could," he agreed. "Or we could talk about your mother."

Her head snapped up, her eyes narrowed as she stared at him. "What do you know about my mother?"

"I know that she makes you sad and that makes me sad," he said simply.

She stared at him for a moment, belligerence

replaced by a kind of wonder. "You mean that, don't you?"

"Do you have to sound so surprised?" he asked, his voice mildly disgruntled. "I may be insincere, but I'm not insensitive."

She smiled. "That pinched, didn't it? I didn't mean to hurt your feelings, but I really don't think you're playing square with Clotilde."

"Chloe. And stop trying to change the subject." He pulled her closer, pushing her head down on his shoulder. "Now, talk," he ordered, his tone uncompromising.

She felt stiff against him for a moment, then she relaxed with a small, heartfelt sigh. "I feel like you're taking my temperature."

"You're stalling."

"I don't know what it is you want me to say," she said, shrugging casually. "I called my mother because it's her birthday."

"And?"

"And what?" she said, shifting away from him only to be pulled back firmly. She sighed heavily. "And we had the same conversation we always have. She asks why I don't call, why I don't care, why I'm not like other women's daughters." She frowned. "She thinks it's my duty to care for her in her old age." She stared up at him, her eyes troubled. "James, she's *forty-three*."

"That's what she thinks," he said gently. "What do you think?"

"Sometimes I feel guilty for having deserted her," she admitted slowly. "But most of the time I just get tired. I get tired of hearing how bad her nerves are. I get tired of hearing how unfair life is and how alone she is. I get tired of hearing how badly everyone treats her." She exhaled wearily. "I just get tired."

"I take it your father is dead."

She nodded. "He died when I was five, but they were divorced two years before that."

"So she should be used to being alone," he said, wanting to say something to take away her feelings of guilt. "Didn't she start some kind of a career after the divorce?"

Dempsey laughed and it was not a pleasant sound. "You might say that," she said stiffly. "She decided to be a professional wife. Her fifth marriage was dissolved three years ago." She glanced up at him. "Before that she didn't care that I didn't live at home. It was only after Fred left that she decided I had deserted her."

"Five times?" he said incredulously.

"That makes her sound frivolous, doesn't it? She's not. She was deadly serious about every single one of her marriages and each of those divorces devastated her. She goes into an old-fashioned decline every time a husband walks out on her. That's when she starts to hold on to me." She was silent for a moment. "It sounds like I'm making light of her problems, but I'm not. She hurts every time. It's easy to say she's setting herself up for misery by continually choosing the wrong man, but that doesn't make it any easier on her. I hate to see her hurting like that."

She closed her eyes and was attacked by visions of her mother, pale and weak, clutching at her, begging her to stop the heartache. Dempsey had opened her heart to the first two stepfathers, but she had ended hating them all—all those nice, average men who had made her mother miserable. And gradually she began to rebel against the inevitability of the hurt.

She would never allow it to happen to her, she had vowed. She decided early that it didn't matter what others did to you. The important thing was how you reacted. Dempsey refused to let circumstances destroy her as they had her mother. She had built a protective barrier because if she didn't take life or people seriously, they couldn't hurt her. She had had enough second-hand pain to last her a lifetime.

Glancing up, she found James staring, not at her face, but at the hands that were clenched, white-knuckled, in her lap. He reached out, placing his hand over hers, and she slowly relaxed her fingers.

"So now you know the sad story of my life. I became a comedienne in self-defense. My own way of rebelling." She grinned. "If my mother had been a jolly woman, I probably would have turned into another Camille."

"Maybe," he said. "I think it more likely that you would still be Dempsey, but without the need to find acceptance in an audience and—"

When he hesitated she raised an arched brow. "And?" she prompted. "Don't stop now. I felt no compunction about telling you you're insincere."

He laughed. "That's true. Okay, I'll say it. I think you look to your audience for love." He felt her stiffen suddenly and knew he had touched a sore spot. "I don't mean to say that you don't relate to people on an individual basis, but from what I've seen, it seems that all you're doing is playing to a smaller audience."

She let out a slow breath. "You mean I'm a fake."

"No, I didn't mean that at all," he denied with a tender smile. "You're very genuine. You simply hide the vulnerable parts behind your natural humor. It's a mechanism. We all have them. They keep us safe."

She stared up at him in inquiry. "What do you hide behind, James?"

"Ambition?" he offered with a shrug. He stood and walked to the window, his thoughts turning sour. "I tell myself I don't need anyone or anything because I have my work." Turning, he looked into her wide gray eyes and knew how much he had been fooling himself.

Desire so strong it rocked his foundations welled up inside him as his eyes drank in the sight of her. He walked back to the bed and sat beside her.

"I was wrong," he murmured, touching her face with an unsteady hand. "I need, Dempsey. *I need.*"

It was an appeal he didn't even try to disguise, and one Dempsey was helpless to resist. Her lips parted in unguarded invitation and, a rough sigh escaping him, his mouth descended. He kissed her like a man starved, starved for love, starved for her.

"Dempsey." His voice was husky with emotion. "I know I'm not the kind of man you usually have a relationship with but"—his hands tightened on her face—"I promise—I promise I know your value. I don't take this lightly."

She didn't hear the words; she felt the emotion, the desperate hunger behind the words, and it was the need to which she responded by arching her body into his, giving him the closeness he was pleading for.

He held her tight, his head back, his eyes closed. "You won't regret it. I promise you that." He opened his eyes and the explosive joy she saw there took her breath away. "Oh, love," he said in a low, hoarse whisper. "I didn't even know how much I needed you until now. I didn't know I was lonely, Dempsey."

The faintly wistful quality in his voice made him sound like a confused little boy. She pulled his head to her breast, holding him tightly. He was pulling up emotions in her she hadn't known existed.

Rolling over, he leaned over her, pushing the strap of her sundress off her shoulder. He brought his lips to the soft, exposed flesh, breathing in her scent.

"How long have I known you, love?" he whispered feverishly against her shoulder.

"Nine days." The words were almost a moan as she moved into his touch.

"It's impossible." He unzipped the dress and drew it down to expose her breasts. "How could this have happened in only nine days? How could I need you so much?"

She watched in mesmerizing silence as his hand moved slowly downward. Taking her nipple into his mouth, he sucked it gently, pulling and teasing it until she was half crazy with desire.

In the moments that followed they entered a world apart, and the isolation of the small compartment served them well. It was as though there had never been a man, had never been a woman, had never been a love until theirs.

Senses heated by anticipation became acute as the unhampered flesh of his hard body moved against the beckoning softness of her own. And the rocking and swaying of the train beneath them became an exquisite part of their pleasure, background music for their sensual song of love. Seeking hands, hungering lips, began a mutual exploration, the tension building with each moment that passed.

"You're so damn beautiful," he said as he stared at her naked body beside him, the intensity in his voice almost painful. "So damn beautiful."

"No . . . *you*," she said urgently, moving her hands across his chest, around his back, and over his hard buttocks. "I'm burning, James," she gasped. "I'm on fire."

He reached down to spread her thighs and she moved against his hand, seeking something to soothe the flames. "We'll fix it, Dempsey," he said hoarsely. "We'll fix it right now."

He slid over her, grasping her buttocks, and every muscle tensed with expectation as he slid inside her body. Suddenly he tensed, stiffening in surprise. "Dempsey," he rasped out. "Why didn't you tell—"

He broke off with a groan as she arched her hips violently and he heard the whimper that was part pain, part pleasure as the full length of him entered the white-hot center of her to put out the flames of aching desire.

"Why didn't you tell me?"

She moved in his arms, her body slippery with perspiration as she stared up through the darkness, trying to read the expression behind the soft question.

"It's not something you advertise," she said wryly. "I hadn't planned on this happening." She reached out to touch his face. "Was it important?"

"I don't know," he said candidly. "I know it's not supposed to be." He paused. "And it's not that I get a kick out of making love to virgins, but . . ." He hesitated, as though having difficulty finding the right words. "But this wasn't a nameless virgin. This was *you*. That makes a difference. And the fact that you've never been with another man is . . . awesome and a little scary. If I had known before, I might have felt inadequate somehow."

"But you didn't know," she said softly. "How do you feel now that it's over?"

"I don't feel that it's over." His voice was husky with emotion. "I feel . . . Oh, I don't know how I feel."

She moved up to kiss him. "As long as you don't feel sorry that it happened."

"Are you kidding?" he asked in astonishment. "Dempsey, there are no words. You know how it usually is to want something. You work your butt off to get it, then somehow it's not what you expected. It's almost as though the wanting is more important than the having." He cradled her close, his hand resting on her breast. "It was not that way with you. The reality surpassed every expectation."

After a moment he said in a strange voice, "And you? Did it live up to your expectations?"

She gave a soft laugh. "You sound like a little boy."

"Do I?" His voice was whimsical. "I don't want us to

get into one of those cliché situations. You know, both of us lying back, smoking cigarettes, and asking, 'Was it good for you?' " She laughed at the image and he continued. "But it would please me to know that you feel the same way I do."

"Then be pleased," she said, propping her elbows on his chest. "I don't know how you can even ask after the way I acted. Now I know what they mean by unbridled passion."

He chuckled. "Yes, you were very much the pagan, weren't you?"

"Now you really sound like a little boy. Very smug. I can feel your chest swelling."

"Times change," he murmured as he pulled her back beside him so that he could lean over her. "Men don't. No matter what century, man's basic needs remain the same."

The last words died away on a whisper as he found her lips, and for a long time their talk was incoherent, but their communication was perfect.

James lay on his back staring at the shadows overhead, feeling the vibration of the moving train. He had told himself that it was all right to make love to her because he was free; he had made no commitments. But he was wrong. He had made commitments, to Dempsey, to himself. Unspoken, but unbreakable commitments.

Now he knew what had been missing in his life. It wasn't children. It wasn't the normalizing institution of marriage. It was love. And love wasn't possible without Dempsey.

He knew he hadn't fallen in love with her simply because he had made love to her. But making love to her had set free the emotions he had been trying to ignore since he had first laid eyes on her. Secretly she had invaded his bloodstream, his mind, his heart. Only he wasn't knowledgeable enough to detect it. He had spent hours wondering what was happening to him, never knowing the answer was as old as man and as natural as spring. He loved.

Suddenly he was bursting with the need to tell her. He raised his head, tenderly gazing down at the woman who slept beside him. He reached out to brush a curl from her cheek, then after a moment he laid his head back on the pillow.

It could wait. His love wasn't going anywhere. It would be with him for the rest of his life. He could wait a few more hours to share it.

Nine

Unshed tears filled Dempsey's closed eyes as his hand touched her cheek. Then he lay back and she felt him relax beside her. For interminable minutes she listened in taut silence until his breathing became deep and even in sleep. Then, careful not to disturb him, she slipped off the bed and began pulling on her clothes.

After tightening the belt of the trench coat, she stared down at him for a moment, then, inhaling a shaky breath, she left the compartment.

She stood in the small area that joined the cars, leaning against the vibrating walls, staring silently at the passing darkness through the small window.

It could have been minutes or hours before the

train finally pulled into a station and slowed to a halt. Slowly, glancing once over her shoulder, Dempsey left the train.

She walked the length of the train, past the engine where men in coveralls busily worked.

"Looks like there'll be a delay."

Raising her eyes from the pavement, she saw a porter she recognized from the train. "I beg your pardon?"

"The train, miss. They're working on it. It'll throw us a little off schedule." He smiled. "So you can take your time inside."

"Oh, I won't be coming back," she said, her smile wistful.

He looked at her curiously. "I thought you were going straight through to Sacramento."

"I changed my mind," she whispered, then turned to walk toward the entrance to the terminal.

Inside, her footsteps echoed eerily in the vast emptiness. She glanced around, then turned to the right when she spotted a small, brightly lit coffee shop.

Except for the waitress, it was as empty as the terminal, but the smell of coffee somehow seemed friendly. She took a seat at the bar, ordering coffee in a subdued tone that would have surprised her friends.

"Waiting for a train?" the waitress asked as she sat the coffee on the counter.

Dempsey looked up, her expression startled, as though she had been awakened suddenly. "I—why, yes, I guess I am," she said. "I'll have to check and see when I can get one back to Los Angeles," she added, speaking more to herself than to the waitress.

"I'm afraid you'll have quite a wait," the thin woman said sympathetically. "The next train for LA won't be through for another two hours."

Dempsey shrugged, then took a sip of coffee. It was strong, hot, and bracing. "I don't mind waiting. I can use some thinking time anyway."

The waitress snorted loudly, leaning against the counter across from her only customer. "Thinking time. I could use some sitting time myself. I'm beat."

Dempsey murmured something she hoped was appropriately understanding as she glanced up at the woman. Although she was extremely thin, she exuded a kind of latent energy. Pulling up a stool behind the white counter, she plopped down and lit a cigarette.

"Does it seem close in here to you?" she asked, then yelled over her shoulder into a back room. "Albert, open that door into the hall, will you? It's close in here." She turned back to Dempsey, fanning her face vigorously with a menu. "Doesn't it seem close in here? Yeah, close," she said again, nodding her head.

Dempsey hid her smile, feeling her mood lighten as she became intrigued by the woman's personality. "Do you work here every night"—she paused to read the name tag pinned to the thin woman's uniform— "Janie."

"Here?" she repeated, lifting one pencil-thin eyebrow. "No way. I couldn't take it. There's not enough business to bother with at night. I usually work days—seven days a week. I like days better." She nodded. "Yeah, days. Always busy." She exhaled a stream of blue smoke. "My usual night job—now, there's a busy place."

"You work two jobs?"

"You bet. For five years now. Keeps me going," she said, chuckling. "You should have seen the party I worked last night. Advertising people," she said with a disgusted snort. "They're all animals. Ate everything in sight. And drink?" She rolled her eyes. "Kept tripping over empty bottles. Dozens of them, laying around like a bunch of dead bodies." She nodded. "Yeah, animals."

Dempsey couldn't hold back a small giggle. "You must have been exhausted."

"Tell me about it. Didn't get out of there till two in the morning."

"How often do you have to work parties?"

"They usually have a dinner a couple of times a week. Big place. Giant place." She nodded. "Yeah, it's big. But parties? They only have them about once a month, thank the good Lord, or they'd kill me for sure."

"And then you have to come in here the next morning?" Dempsey asked in amazement.

"Seven days a week," she confirmed proudly. "Twelve hours a day."

"You're incredible," Dempsey said, truly awed.

Janie nodded with no show of false modesty. "It's a good life. I don't have to answer to anyone about how I spend my money." She leaned closer. "I took a cruise last summer and this year I'm going skiing. I got a mink coat that I paid for myself." She stared up at the ceiling. "It's a good life. No one to let down. No one to let me down. Just me." She nodded. "Yeah, it's good."

No one to let down. No one to answer to, Dempsey thought as Janie turned to wait on a new customer. That was what Dempsey wanted. She wanted no ties. She didn't want to be serious, and what she had just experienced with James felt serious.

Resting her chin on her hands, Dempsey stared at the dusty picture of the Golden Gate Bridge that hung behind the counter, her gray eyes troubled. How could she have let it happen? She had known that first night that he was not the kind of man she could have as a friend. In every way they were too far apart. Then when they had come so close to loving on his couch, she had felt a crippling panic at the thought of becoming involved with him.

But she had fooled herself when she thought she had escaped involvement. In an incredibly short amount of time he had become completely enmeshed in her life. She felt as though she had made a promise tonight, a promise she hadn't intended and didn't want to keep.

She inhaled a shaky breath. Perhaps she was overreacting, she thought in panicky silence. The first time was supposed to be traumatic.

But her natural honesty forced her to admit that making love with James hadn't felt in the least traumatic. It had felt wonderful and warm and absolutely right. And that was the problem. This wasn't something she would forget about next week. This was serious, dammit!

". . . and you can bring me a piece of that apple pie if it's not too much trouble, my dear."

Dempsey's head jerked up abruptly. She knew that voice. Twisting the stool to the side, she turned to stare at the short, bald man and gasped, "Mac! For heaven's sake, what are you doing here?"

His blue eyes opened wide. "Dempsey, darling girl!" He stood and came close to give her an exuberant hug. "Imagine running into you here."

"Yes, but why are you here?"

"Relatives, dear, relatives," he said, waving the question away. "You know what a headache they are. But I never expected to see my favorite person in a strange train station in the middle of the night. What brings you to this out-of-the-way place?"

She shrugged. "I'm just passing through on my way back to LA."

He trained his penetrating eyes on her face, studying her features for a long, uncomfortable moment. "Is something wrong, Dempsey? Your lovely face is usually so animated, so alive. I've never seen you looking so *serious*."

She winced at the sound of the awful word, then looked up to smile brightly. "Are you kidding? Me, serious? Not—" She swallowed heavily. "Not very likely. Your age must finally be getting to your eyes, Mac."

"We'll leave my age out of this, please," he said with dignity, turning to thank Janie for the pie and coffee. "Yes, I can see I was mistaken," he said reflectively after taking a large bite of the pie. "My Dempsey wouldn't be serious about anything."

"That's right," she said, unaware of the belligerence of her tone. "Life's for having fun." She leaned closer to whisper confidingly, "Earnestness is the pits, Mac."

He nodded in agreement. "You've got the right of it there, love. And no one knows how to avoid it better than you. Not only that, but you can turn a situation around completely. Your ingenuity always amazes me. If things look like they're getting earnest and grim, you simply work your special magic and before you know it everything's lighthearted and just for fun. You're not one to be beaten by a little earnestness. No, sir."

Dempsey had been playing with her spoon as he spoke, then slowly her moody expression changed and the smile that curved her lips was natural, her eyes surprised.

"You're right," she said, sitting up straight. "An affair—a situation gets serious only if you let it. Why didn't I think of that?"

She didn't have to panic over her relationship with James, she thought with pleasure. She could make it anything she wanted it to be. She could stay with him as she was aching to do; she would simply keep the affair in perspective.

"Mac, you're an angel," she said, kissing him soundly. "I owe you one for this."

"What ever are you talking about?" he said, blue eyes twinkling.

"I'll explain it to you later," she said vaguely, her mind caught up in the relief of not having to leave James. She could sneak back into the compartment without his knowing that she had left. And she would take care to keep from him the fact that she had ever had such doubts about their relationship. She would stay on the train for as long—

"Omigosh," she gasped. "The train!" Jumping up, she looked around for Mac, but except for Janie, the room was empty.

Shaking her head, she called a hasty good-bye to the waitress and ran out of the coffee shop. The empty terminal seemed larger than before as she ran across it, her heart pounding with an unexplainable fear. At last she gained the door and swung around it—just as the train began to pull away.

She stood in motionless silence, her breathing raspy, her chest tight with an unfamiliar pain, and watched the train pass, its closed doors dismally final.

She was too late, she thought numbly. Then her eyes widened as she saw a door open and the porter she had spoken to earlier stood just inside, beckoning her frantically.

"Come on, miss," he called as the train began to pick up speed. "I'll help you."

Without hesitation Dempsey ran. She ran as though her life depended on it, without understanding why it was so desperately important that she catch the train.

"You can make it, miss," the porter called, extending his hand to her. "You can make it. Give me your hand."

Her lungs felt like bursting, but she couldn't give up. Reaching out to him, she pulled up every ounce of strength she possessed. Then she felt his fingers touch hers. Making a small sound of triumph, she held tightly and felt herself being hauled aboard.

A few seconds later she leaned against the wall, her breathing harsh. She closed her eyes and let relief wash over her. Glancing up, her eyes met those of the porter, and suddenly they both began to laugh.

"I didn't think you were going to make it, miss," he said. "You must be in good shape."

"Are you kidding?" she said, her eyes sparkling. "You're talking to an ex-guard with the Blue Lake Debs basketball team. It was a piece of cake," she finished airily, then moaned as her knees began to collapse.

Thanking the porter in breathless but heartfelt tones, she made her way back to the compartment. James was still sleeping soundly when she entered silently. She smiled down at him, taking a moment just to study his face.

In repose, the strong, harsh lines were softened. Or perhaps what they had shared had softened her image of him. No longer was he a stiff, uncompromising executive. He was a man who was very much a man but who could also be tender and loving in a way that would melt the hardest heart. How could she have ever thought his face forbidding? she wondered in amazement. His gentle spirit was written all over his face and contained in the compassionate strength of his hands.

She felt her heart swell, and slowly she began to remove her clothes. When she slid into bed beside him, he turned to her in his sleep, enfolding her in his arms as though they had been together for years.

"Dempsey," he said sleepily.

"Yes, darling?" she whispered.

She could feel him come awake and smiled when he whispered, "Nothing. Just . . . Dempsey."

She gave a soft laugh, turning so that she could see his face. When she reached out to caress the familiar features, he caught her hand, bringing it to his lips.

"I had the silliest dream," he whispered into her palm.

"Mmmm?" she said dreamily.

"I dreamed I couldn't find you. I knew it was just a dream. I knew if I woke up you would be here, but I couldn't wake up." He brought her hand to his chest, spreading the fingers and pressing it close. "I'm glad I woke up."

"Yes," she whispered intensely. "Yes, so am I."

She buried her face in his neck, feeling the compelling warmth, and moved against him hungrily, needing to forget how close she had come to letting this go.

His hands slid over her body, and as though he had read her mind, he began to love her again.

Ten

"Something very weird is going on, James."

Dempsey sat beside him in the cab, staring at the pleased expression on his face. He had been acting peculiar since he had awakened that morning. And to confuse her even more, when the porter had delivered another envelope, James had simply shoved it into his pocket. As soon as the train had arrived in Sacramento, he had pulled her through the terminal and into a cab before she could catch her breath.

She slowly shook her finger in accusation. "Where are we going and why didn't you read the note?"

"I don't need to read it," he said, a smile lighting his dark eyes.

"Well, I know it's lousy poetry, but those notes are

our only clues." When he chuckled, she said, "Let me guess. Last night you slipped into a deep coma and when you woke up you found"—she paused to open her eyes wide and whistle the theme from "The Twilight Zone"—"you found that you had contracted the dreaded esp."

"Esp?" he repeated, choking on the word.

"Extra whatever whatever," she explained, dismissing it with a wave of her hand. "So you know what the note says without opening it. What was it? 'By the shores of Sacramento. By the shining metal factories' . . . something like that?"

He pulled her arm through his and leaned back in the seat, smiling in content. "I don't know what was in the note and I don't care," he said smugly.

She opened her eyes wide. "My, my. Aren't we complacent? What happened to you? This can't be the same man who eats, drinks, and sleeps business. Is the rising young executive shirking his duty?" She squealed when he pinched her nose, then she examined his face. "I can't believe you really aren't going to look at that note."

"I don't need to look at it." He glanced down as he very casually played with her fingers.

"Why not?" she asked suspiciously. "You've certainly been hot to get all the others."

"I don't need to look at the note because last night I thought of something—in between the times I was thinking of you," he added. "That non-word you were making fun of—circumambulatory. That's the clue. To circumambulate means to walk in circles."

"You looked it up," she accused.

"No, I didn't," he said, chuckling. "I simply broke it down into its respective parts and analyzed it. It was no problem once I—"

"James, dear," she interrupted dryly, "you can give me an English lesson some other time. Just tell me what the clue means."

"It means that Uncle Charlie will give me the papers as soon as we get back to LA."

"Why have we traveled all over California if the papers were in Los Angeles?"

"Being able to understand Uncle Charlie scares the hell out of me," he said ruefully, "but I think he sent me off with you to get my mind off business. He must have been watching that night in the alley and knew you were beginning to get under my skin."

She gave him a coy look. "Am I doing that?"

"You know damn well you are," he said, leaning over to nip her ear in punishment.

She chuckled. "I told you I liked your uncle. He sounds like a wonderful man."

"He sounds like a nut," James muttered. "Anyway, as long as I don't have to worry about those diagrams, I can relax," he finished with a pleased smile.

She studied him silently for a moment. "Ah-ha!" she said suddenly, causing him to jump and stare at her. "I knew there was something fishy about the way you were acting. You were trying to make me believe that you had turned over a new leaf and were going to forget all about work. Trying to kid a kidder, James?"

He grinned down at her. "Forgetting about business is just exactly what I'm doing, so don't sound so smug."

"Oh, yeah?" she said, shaking her head. "Well, I'll believe it when I see it. And you still haven't told me where we're going."

"That's right, I haven't," he agreed. "We are playing hookey. From duty, responsibility, and that little devil, ambition."

She smiled at him virtuously. "While I concede that you need a vacation from each and all of those things, I don't happen to be caught in that particular trap."

"Oh, no? You, my dear, are caught in exactly the same trap." He raised a hand to stop her indignant protest. "You are as dedicated to your work as I am to mine. The minute you walk onstage, the world can go hang as far as you're concerned. You are totally, completely, involved in your career." He eyed her sternly. "And don't tell me you don't have ambitions, because I won't believe you."

"All right already," she said in grudging surrender. "So we're both caught up in our careers. That doesn't tell me where we're going."

"We're going to have fun," he said, smiling in pleasure. "We're going to spend the day in museums."

She fell silent from surprise, then glanced at him from the corners of her eyes. "Museums . . . fun?" she said, her voice faint. "Gee, James, I don't know if my heart can stand that much excitement." She turned to stare at him inquisitively. "Is that honestly what you do for fun?"

"What's wrong with it?" he asked indignantly.

"Nothing," she hastened to assure him. "Nothing at all, but—"

"But?"

She turned sideways in the seat to face him. "Why don't you let me be your guide to fun? I mean, this is something I know. If you want to know about porpoises, you wouldn't go to someone who specializes in iguanas, would you? You would go to a porpoise expert. If you want to know about fun"—she smiled modestly—"you come to me."

Pulling her closer, he gazed reflectively at her delicate face. After a moment he said, "That makes damn good sense. All right, I'm placing myself in your capable hands. Do with me what you will."

She reached up lovingly to stroke his angular jaw. "What an intriguing invitation," she murmured. "All kinds of possibilities spring to mind."

A fire blazed in his eyes and his arms closed around her, but when he dipped his head, she ducked under his arm, laughing at his thwarted expression as she knocked on the glass that separated them from the driver.

"Dempsey." James's voice was wary as he stared in astonishment. "Dempsey Turner-Riley, what have you gotten me into?"

"Did you or did you not place yourself in my hands, my *capable* hands?" she asked, pulling him toward the log ride that sat in the center of the giant amusement park.

He hung back, still eyeing the curving, swooping water-filled trough. "I said that," he said vaguely, shaking his head as though he doubted his sanity. "Yes, I actually said that. But is this"—he gestured toward the ride—"really necessary? Couldn't we compromise?"

"Compromise? Next you'll be wanting to hold a board meeting and appoint a committee to discuss it. Come on, don't be chicken-hearted."

His skeptical gaze followed a group of people leaving the ride. "Dempsey, those people are wet."

"You're really going to love this, James. It will put the roses back in your cheeks."

"They're *wet*," he said faintly.

"We'll be just like Tom Sawyer floating down the old Mississippi. Riding the rapids and—"

"*Dripping* wet."

She stopped walking suddenly and stared up at him. "James," she said firmly. "No matter what all those smitten women have told you over the years, you are not so sweet that a little water will melt you."

Amusement appeared in his dark eyes as his gaze met and held hers. "Oh, no?" he said with deliberation, jerking her close to kiss her soundly.

After a moment she opened her eyes. "Well," she said huskily, "maybe I'll lend you my trench coat."

He laughed. "Come on. If we're going to do this, let's get it over with."

As they walked toward the ride, Dempsey had a strange notion. The sun shining down on them, the fresh warmth of the air, the day was so special, it almost seemed as though they had a guardian angel watching out for them to insure that their day of escape was perfect.

She glanced up to mention the thought to James,

then shook her head. It was too fantastical to say out loud.

She grinned suddenly, watching his wary expression as they got nearer the ride. She had a feeling she was going to enjoy this very much.

James grumbled through the first two curves of the ride, but when he saw water clinging like a sprinkling of diamonds to her dark curls and dripping from her delicate nose, he pulled Dempsey back between his thighs and she could feel his rumbling laughter against her back.

From that moment on, James took charge of their escapade. With careful advice from the expert, he led their expedition to a Little League baseball game in the park and on a hilarious tour of a beer-bottling factory. It was as though he had rediscovered his childhood. And experiencing it with the worldly knowledge of an adult served only to make it more wonderful.

Later he grinned as he stared at her back. He was catching on fast, he thought. A few more lessons and he would have the fun thing down pat.

"Just remember," she called over her shoulder, the bicycle beneath her wobbling, "this little venture was your idea."

He sped by her. "If anyone comes to grief, it will be you. At least I'm dressed for it."

She glanced at his knit sport shirt and slacks, then down at her own short sundress. "I'm wearing my train outfit," she said, puffing slightly. "You didn't say anything about riding bicycles."

"It was an inspiration from heaven," he said,

laughing. "I haven't ridden a bicycle in years. I had forgotten how much fun they were until I saw the rental stand."

"Inspiration from heaven, my foot," she scoffed. "God has more sense."

"You're miffed just because you know you're out of shape. It's all that night life," he warned. "It'll get you every time."

She pulled her bike off the track and pedaled toward a group of trees that looked like a perfect spot for lunch. "Don't sound so smug. Don't try to tell me that you get any exercise other than in a gym. I'd bet that even your tan is canned."

"Then you'd be wrong," he said. He stepped off his bike and fixed the kickstand, then pulled her away from hers and into his arms. "The company has a beach house that I use. Lots of sand and sun and ocean."

"You're the original beach bum, all right," she said, laughing as she slipped out of his arms to open the bag that contained the food.

James couldn't take his eyes off Dempsey. He had found a miracle, a miracle in the shape of a woman. He knew now that all those years he hadn't been living at all. He had simply existed. He had been a euphemism, a polite substitution for the real thing. Loving Dempsey had brought him to life. She made the world shine for him and he felt his love for her growing and swelling, spilling over in laughter and boundless enthusiasm for life.

He was waiting for just the right moment to tell her. That would make his happiness complete. He would devote the rest of his life to loving Dempsey. And every minute of every day he would try to repay her for what she had given him.

"Hey," she said, drawing him out of his reverie.

She sat beside him in the cab that was taking them back to the train station after a very full, very special day.

"Don't just sit there and look cute," she continued. "Do something constructive."

He raised a questioning brow. "Such as?"

Slipping out of her shoes, she placed her feet in his lap. "Such as rubbing my feet," she said, sighing. "I feel like someone peeled the skin off inch by inch with a dull knife, then took a cigarette lighter—"

"God, but you have a way with words." He grimaced as he rubbed her feet. "Sometimes your imagination is too much for my stomach."

"Mmmm. That feels gorgeous. I'll do yours as soon as we get back on the train." She raised her head from the seat back. "Why are we going by train back to LA? We could take a plane and be there in no time."

"True," he said, smiling to himself as he concentrated on her other foot. "But I've grown rather fond of trains." He slid his hand up her calf and over her knee, sending delicious shivers deep inside her. "There's something about the vibrations beneath you when you're lying naked with a small, warm woman in your arms."

Dempsey sucked in a stunned breath, heat flooding her body at the vivid picture he conjured up. "You—you have a way with words yourself," she gasped.

The sensuous sound of his laughter filled the cab.

Pulling her into his arms, he felt the desire trembling in her limbs and wished desperately that they were already alone in a tiny train compartment.

When they arrived at the terminal, he kept his arm around her and walked with her toward the trains. Suddenly he frowned, his steps slowing.

Dempsey glanced up at him in inquiry. "Is there something wrong?"

"Yes," he said slowly, then more firmly, "yes, there is. I need to make a call."

Doubling back, he found the line of pay telephones. He lifted a receiver and punched in his credit card number as Dempsey watched him in confusion.

"Sounds important," she said quietly.

He smiled at the curiosity in her voice. He would tell her about it later. He would tell her everything later. All about his sudden need to clear away the past. About his desire to be square with Chloe at last. He had to make sure she wouldn't be hurt by his new happiness.

Dempsey leaned against the wall, whistling through her teeth as she examined her fingernails. She knew the phone call was to his blond friend, and Dempsey was trying very hard not to be too interested. He spoke in low tones, then in a surprisingly short time, hung up the telephone and turned away, smiling broadly as his eyes met hers.

"Good news?" she asked with studied nonchalance.

"You could say that," he said casually. "Chloe agrees with you."

"That's nice." She frowned, her brow creasing in thought. "About what?"

"About me." He chuckled. "She thinks she deserves better than me too."

Dempsey stared up at him, her eyes sparkling with indignation. "Well—well, of all the nerve!" she sputtered angrily. "I hope she just tries to find better. Where does she get off—"

"Hold on," he said, smiling with pleasure at the way she leaped instantly to his defense. What Chloe had actually said was that she was going to try to find someone who would look at her the way James looked at Dempsey. Chloe was one smart lady, he decided.

"You can't trust blondes," Dempsey said with undisguised belligerence. "Something in the hair pigment goes to their brains. She's obviously a little slow."

He laughed. "But you said the same thing," he reminded her.

"That's different," she mumbled defensively.

"Come on," he said, hiding his smile. "We've got a train to catch."

They had dinner in the dining car again, talking in sudden bursts of enthusiasm. Then just as suddenly they would fall silent, each knowing the other was thinking of the bed that waited for them in a gently rocking room. Of limbs entwined and worlds left behind.

As they walked along the corridor toward their compartment, neither of them gave more than a second's notice to a small man with center-parted hair and a handlebar mustache who watched their progress with twinkling blue eyes.

James opened the door for Dempsey, then followed

her inside, leaning against it for a moment. He had suddenly realized that the time was right at last. He couldn't go any longer without telling her what was in his mind, in his heart.

Eleven

Dempsey sat on the bed and began to remove her shoes. She was tired but exhilarated. Today she had seen a James she hadn't known existed. It was a day out of time, one she would treasure for the rest of her life. No matter where their separate lives led them, she would always have the memory of this day to hold on to.

Her lazy movements stopped, her heart jerking in her breast as she thought ahead to the end of their affair. It was a reaction with which she was becoming familiar, and it worried her. She had to remember that she was in control of her emotions. She was in no danger as long as she kept it light.

Lifting her eyes, she found James watching her

and an uncontrollable smile stretched her lips. "Come here," she ordered, jerking her head to the side.

His lips quivered in amusement as he moved his head slowly from side to side.

"Hmmmm," she murmured thoughtfully. "Playing hard to get, are we?" She motioned again, winking cockily. "I said, come here."

Suddenly he took two large steps and was reaching down to pull her into his arms. "I'm crazy," he whispered huskily against her cheek.

"Possibly," she agreed amiably, playing with the muscles in his neck. "But so is everybody, so who's to notice?"

Catching her shoulders, he pulled her away so that he could look into her eyes. "I'm crazy about you, Dempsey." He inhaled shakily, the intensity in his face almost painful to witness. "Dempsey, I've got so much to tell you."

She stared at him in curiosity. There was a feverish look about him that bothered her, and she had never seen him look so vulnerable.

"Come," he said. "Let's sit down." He ran a hand through his hair and gave a small, mocking laugh. "There's so much. When I think of what I was and where I was going, it all seems inconceivable now. And the wild part is, I thought I was happy." He shook his head in bewilderment. "I actually thought I was happy."

The smile on her face slipped as she watched him, and some of her color faded away. She made a small, protesting motion with her hand, but he was too caught up with his own thoughts to notice.

"Uncle Charlie tried to tell me," he continued avidly. "But I wouldn't listen. I wasn't able to understand—then." He sat down beside her, picking up her hands to hold them tightly between his. "That's another miracle to your credit. You gave me the ability to see the truth."

"No—" she began in desperation, but he stopped her before she could continue.

"Wait, let me tell you." He smiled down at her tenderly, his lips trembling slightly. "I've never been a bad person, Dempsey. Not truly. I had a rigid code of ethics to which I adhered. But—but without knowing it I became so absorbed in my narrow world that I saw other people only as figures I could arrange at convenient positions around that world." He leaned closer, his eyes on fire with emotion. "Don't you see? I wasn't letting anyone in to share it with me. Uncle Charlie saw that. He tried to tell me how much I was missing, but I couldn't see."

His hand shook when he lifted it to her face. "I refused to see until I met you." He closed his eyes and a small laugh escaped him. "Lord, you broke through the barriers without even trying. And suddenly I could see. It all became clear. Not only did you step through, but you brought the world in with you. I'm aware, really aware, of people and things for the first time in years. I'm more truly alive than I've ever been. This is what Uncle Charlie wanted for me. This is what I wanted for myself without even knowing it. I was determined to marry the 'right' person. I thought that would make my life complete." He smiled. "When I met you I wanted to have an affair with you and *then* marry the 'right' person. It took me a while to see that there would be no contentment, no life without you."

"James, please." The words were almost a groan.

"Let me finish, Dempsey. I've waited too long to tell you." He inhaled roughly. "Now that I've got up the courage, let me tell it all. I want you to know how much you've given me. You've even redefined the meaning of love for me. Before, I thought that falling in love was finding someone who shared your interests, someone with whom you could coexist comfortably." He laughed again at himself. "Comfortably. What an insipid word. Loving is not like that at all. It makes all your senses come alive. It makes a sunrise or a bottling factory the most exciting thing in the world. And you did it, Dempsey. You did that for me. Without you I wouldn't have known."

He ran his thumb across her lips. "Loving you is the best thing that ever happened to me, Dempsey. And if you'll let me, I'll spend the rest of my life showing you how much you mean to me." He leaned his forehead against hers. "Let's get married soon, Dempsey. It will be so wonderful. I want to show you how—"

Suddenly a low moan escaped her and she jerked away from him, her eyes taking on a hunted look. "No," she whispered. "No more."

As she stood up and moved away from the bed, she saw confusion spread across his face, but she couldn't let it affect her.

"You've got to stop this, James," she said with

feverish intensity. "You're letting things get out of proportion. You see"—she paused to swallow roughly—"you see, what's happened here is that you expected me to be experienced. Then when you found out I was a virgin, you—you felt some kind of misplaced responsibility." She tried to smile. "It's not necessary, James. I knew what I was doing."

He laughed in relief. "Is that what's bothering you? Well, you can forget it. I fell in love with you a long time before we made love. I just didn't recognize it. I—"

"No! Don't say any more. You don't know what you're talking about. There's no way we can get married," she said, her eyes desperate.

"What are you saying?"

She sat down beside him and picked up his hand, unaware of how her nails dug into him. "You're not thinking logically. I'm just for fun, remember? You're talking about something that I don't know anything about . . . and don't want to know," she added firmly, as though trying to convince herself. "How could we possibly make a go of marriage? We're as different as two people can be. You're museums; I'm amusement parks. You're imported Scotch; I'm beer and peanuts. And look at our careers. They don't mesh. I work nights. How could I raise a family?" She gave a short laugh. "Family? Can you imagine me with kids? I'd be a terrible mother. And I couldn't give up my work. Not for anyone."

"I'm not asking you to." He stared at her silently for long, tense moments. "Our careers are not the problem. You know we could work something out. And neither is your ability to be a good mother. I've seen you with Irene's kids. Whatever you're trying to say, Dempsey, just say it," he said quietly. "But you're going to have a tough time convincing me that it won't work. I know it will."

She laughed shakily, running a hand across her hair. "You're kidding me again, aren't you? You know this reminds me of the time—"

"Don't make jokes!" he said harshly. "I want you to be serious for once."

Her smile trembled as she whispered, "But I don't know how, James." The words hung for a moment in silence before she continued. "I've never known. It always makes me uncomfortable." She turned away sharply. "Anytime there is trouble or tragedy, don't look for me, because I always play least in sight." Her voice was barely audible when she added, "I'm just for fun, James. Don't you know that?"

He walked to her, holding her gently by the shoulders. "All you have to do is be yourself, Dempsey."

She laughed again. "And have everyone run and hide? No, I can't do that. I don't even know if I could find me."

"I can," he said softly. "If you'll let me try. We could do it together. In the past two days, Dempsey, I've seen pieces of the real you. That has to mean something."

For a moment she sagged weakly, then she moved away from him. "No." She shook her head frantically. "You've got to stop this. It won't work, because I won't marry you." She inhaled, then spoke through clenched teeth. "What can I say to convince you?"

Looking into his eyes, she said deliberately, "I couldn't possibly marry you, James, because I don't love you."

His head jerked back as though she had struck him. For endless moments he sat motionless, his face pale and drained of all emotion. The room was heavy with tension as the silence dragged out. Then suddenly he began to laugh, an ugly sound that made her flinch away from him.

"By God, it serves me right," he said, his voice harsh. "I was so wrapped up in the wonder of what was happening to me, it never occurred to me that you didn't feel it too. How could I be so naive? I thought it was too strong to be one-sided." He shook his head. "Like I said, love, you're teaching me all kinds of new things."

"James, I'm sorry—" she began hesitantly.

"No, it's all right." He seemed dazed as he shook his head, smiling slightly. "You shouldn't ever apologize for telling the truth." His voice drifted away and he turned to stare out the window at the passing night. "We should be in LA in a couple of hours," he said conversationally.

"I—I think I'll ride the rest of the way in the day coach," she said, her voice constricted. "I'll probably see you at the station."

"Sure," he said vaguely. "You go ahead."

The rest of the trip was a private and separate hell for each of them. But as the miles sped by, bringing them closer to the end of their incredible journey, their thoughts were closer than either of them knew.

When the train slowed and stopped at last,

Dempsey was one of the first to depart. She thought if only she could get back to her own world, she would be all right. She would forget the past two days. She would forget the look on his face.

Her hands clenched into tight, hard fists as she walked, and she knew she would never forget. It would always be with her. She would never be able to close her eyes without seeing again the way he looked when she had told him that she didn't love him.

"Dempsey! Dempsey, wait."

No more, she begged silently when she heard James's voice. Please, no more.

Grasping her arm, he pulled her to a halt, then guided her away from the stream of travelers leaving the train. His face looked older somehow and unutterably weary.

"I've got to talk to you."

She moved her head miserably from side to side. "Why, James?" she whispered. "Why do we have to drag it out? We've said it all."

He shook her roughly. "No, dammit! We haven't said it all." Pushing her against the wall, he leaned over her, trapping her. "I did a lot of thinking after you left, Dempsey, and it just won't wash." He touched her face. "You're a sensitive woman. If you honestly didn't love me, you would have done everything in your power to keep from hurting me." He stared into her frightened eyes. "That wasn't the case, was it? You intentionally hurt me. That means you love me and are fighting the way you feel."

She shook her head frantically in denial. "No—"

"*Yes*," he insisted, giving her another shake. "You

love me, but you're afraid. You're afraid you'll end up like your mother. You would rather let life, real life, pass you by than take a chance on being hurt. You're hiding from love behind fun and games."

"You don't know *anything*," she spat out.

"I know you're a coward. I know you think you get all you need from your audience." He grasped her chin roughly, forcing her to meet his eyes. "It may have worked before, Dempsey, but try it now. You see if all those invisible people can give you what you need. But don't be surprised if it's different now. You've had the real thing . . . and you're going to find out that love's a tough act to follow."

She jerked her head out of his hands. She had to get away from him. She couldn't let him mess up her mind with lies. Without a word she walked away, mingling quickly with the crowd headed for the street entrance to the terminal.

James felt his last ounce of hope drain from him as she walked away. He had given it his best shot and he had lost.

"I'm sorry, James."

The quiet voice came from just beside him, and James glanced down to find his uncle standing next to him. "Hello, Uncle Charlie," he said, too empty to even wonder about his presence.

"I accomplished what I wanted to accomplish," the older man said softly. "But I didn't mean for it to be like this. I meant it for the best." He shook his head, then handed his nephew a manila envelope. "Here are your papers, son."

"Thanks, Uncle Charlie," he murmured, his eyes

trained on a figure that was getting smaller and smaller.

Dempsey kept her head down as she walked. She felt pursued—pursued by his eyes, by her own thoughts. Unexplainably, the waitress, Janie, popped into her mind. No one to answer to, she had said. No one. Just me. That had sounded so right at the time. Why did it now sound sad?

James was wrong, she told herself defiantly. He had to be. She simply couldn't love him. She simply . . .

But she did, she admitted wearily. It had been there for a long time, way in the back of her mind, in the bottom of her heart. Maybe it had been there that first night.

And he was also right about her being afraid. What would happen to her if she let him into her life and then he decided to leave? Wouldn't she turn into a younger version of her mother? Heredity and environment combined to work against her. She couldn't face that kind of future.

So what's your future like now? she thought suddenly. What kind of future did she face without James? Love's a tough act to follow, he had said. And she could see nothing ahead that would come even close to what she felt when she was with him.

Her steps slowed, then stopped, and people pushed into her from behind as his words finally got through to her. Turning quickly, she searched through the crowd around her. She had to find him. She had to tell him that she knew now. She knew that she wouldn't really be alive unless she took a chance on their love. She had had a vision of her life without James, and it had felt empty.

Suddenly she saw him, still standing where she had left him earlier. Mac was beside him, but there wasn't room in her mind to find that odd. Going against the stream of people, she began to push through the crowd, oblivious to the irritable stares that were directed at her. She moved faster and faster, impatient now to tell him of her love. She would make it up to him. She would take away the pain she had caused if he would let her. As long as she lived, she never wanted to see such a look on his face, and she would do anything in her power to prevent it.

Her heart was pounding, her eyes anxious as she almost ran toward the other side of the room, murmuring hasty apologies as she knocked into people. Then he saw her, saw her fighting to get to him, and slowly his face changed. The dreadful weariness disappeared and was replaced by such a magnificent joy, the sight of it brought the sting of tears to her eyes.

"Dempsey," he whispered hoarsely, and moved out into the crowd, the manila envelope slipping unnoticed to the floor.

He moved roughly past the people in his way, allowing nothing to slow him down. Within seconds he had her in his arms and knew he would never let her go again.

"I'm sorry, James," she said, her words as frantic as the kisses she spread on his face.

"No, don't," he said, shaking his head slightly. "I

shouldn't have sprung it on you like that. I shouldn't have assumed you wanted to marry me."

"But I do," she cried. "More than anything in the world. I'll quit my job at the Green Duck. I'll stay home and scrub floors and cook meat loaf and have dozens and dozens of children. Anything," she whispered. "Just as long as I can be with you. Don't let me go, James. Don't let me go."

"Never," he said, laughing shakily. "And I won't let you give up your career. You're too talented, Dempsey. You can't give it up. Our kids will just have to be night people so that they can see their mother perform."

She framed his face with her hands. "James, I love you." When he drew in a sharp breath, she knew how much the words meant, and she said them over and over again.

For a long time they stood, wrapped in each other's arms, wrapped in each other's hearts.

Bending down, a small, bald man picked up the forgotten manila envelope, then stood watching them with satisfaction sparkling in his clear sky-blue eyes. Neither paid attention when he muttered smugly, "I told them so. By George, I told them so."

THE EDITOR'S CORNER

Next month should be called "Especially Fabulous Reading Month!" Not only is Bantam publishing four marvelous LOVESWEPTS (of course) and Sandra Brown's sensational sequel to **SUNSET EMBRACE, ANOTHER DAWN,** but also we are reissuing Celeste DeBlasis's extraordinary novel, **THE PROUD BREED.**

An excerpt from ANOTHER DAWN follows this Editor's Corner; next month you can look forward to an excerpt from **THE PROUD BREED.** I know you're going to enjoy both of these longer novels very, very much. By the way, some booksellers display books like **ANOTHER DAWN** and **THE PROUD BREED** in general fiction or in special displays in areas of their stores where you might not think to look for them. So, if you don't see these novels right away, do make a special point of asking your bookseller for them.

Now for those Fabulous Four LOVESWEPTS coming next month.

Sara Orwig creates for all of us a mellow, yet thrilling romance, **DEAR MIT,** LOVESWEPT #111. Just think of the nostalgic pleasure of receiving a letter from your very best friend (and very best tormentor) throughout childhood with whom you've lost touch. Then add that in the present that friend is a thoroughly adult male and a very amusing correspondent who hasn't forgotten a thing about you. Now you're ready to put yourself in heroine Marilyn Pearson's place and imagine her response when at last she encounters Colly face-to-face and finds him devastatingly attractive. And the feeling is definitely mutual. "Mellow," "nostalgic," or any other kind of tame emotion flies right out the window then and it's all sparks and fire between them. But their lives have developed along diverse paths and seem impossible to meld—except perhaps when they stand together beneath the old

(continued)

pear tree that was their special childhood spot. . . . Well, we'll keep you guessing about what happens there, but we won't keep you in suspense about our feeling that **DEAR MIT** is one of Sara's most original, funny, and endearing romances ever!

Given your wonderfully warm welcome for Peggy Webb's first romance, **TAMING MAGGIE,** LOVE- SWEPT #106, I know you'll be very pleased to learn that she has another book coming up next month, **BIRDS OF A FEATHER,** LOVESWEPT #112. In this delectable story, young widow Mary Ann Gilcrest finds herself—much to her dismay and her mother's delight— in the midst of a birdwatchers' retreat. But suddenly it isn't such a dismal event; as a matter of fact it becomes a downright wonderful one! And the not-so-simple reason for the change in Mary Ann's view is magnificent Bill Benson. Alas, their days together in the wilderness are over much too soon and they must go their separate ways. Then Bill promises forever, but she can't believe in their future together. Bill's relentless pursuit causes a furor to break out in her hometown . . . and the most charming madness surrounds this wonderful couple in an ending to **BIRDS OF A FEATHER** that you aren't likely to forget!

And next we have a sensitive, most imaginative author joining us, Linda Hampton, with **A MATTER OF MAGIC,** LOVESWEPT #113. Linda's delightful debut book with LOVESWEPT features the most romantic sleight-of-hand from a marvelous hero, Murray Richards. How he impresses heroine Georgette Finlay when he helps her retrieve a pile of dropped packages and then produces a rose from thin air! Georgette feels it is truly providential that they met because she's a talent agent who's been scouting long and hard for a magician. She does a hard sell job on Murray—but he isn't buying! Magic is strictly a hobby for the high-powered executive. No, he wants a far different relationship with Georgette . . . but will he pull it off only by using every trick of the illusionist's trade to weave a spell of sensual enchantment around her? Getting the answer to that question is getting a sure-fire treat in romantic reading!

Be sure to have a box of tissues nearby when you pick up Joan Elliott Pickart's **RAINBOW'S ANGEL**, LOVESWEPT #114, because this lovely story is probably going to bring tears of sentiment and laughter to your eyes. The hero is the debonair R. J. Jenkins from **SUNLIGHT'S PROMISE** and from the moment he lays eyes on Kelly Morgan he's a goner! Their first encounter takes his breath away . . . their next meeting impresses him with her business acumen . . . their third meeting melts his heart. Kelly touches R. J. as no woman ever has with her beauty, brains, courage, and heart. But they have so little time together and R. J. has to make many difficult decisions before he can commit to Kelly, the adoring mother of toddler Sara. **RAINBOW'S ANGEL** is one of Joan's most touching, truly emotional love stories.

We hope you'll agree with us that the four LOVE-SWEPTs along with **ANOTHER DAWN** and **THE PROUD BREED** add up to "Especially Fabulous Reading Month" from Bantam Books.

With every warm wish,

Sincerely,

Carolyn Nichols

Carolyn Nichols
  Editor
LOVESWEPT
Bantam Books, Inc.
666 Fifth Avenue
New York, NY 10103

J ake followed Banner into the living room. He trod lightly, like a convict who had just been granted a stay of execution. She seemed tranquil enough, but he didn't trust her mood. He had meddled in her business when she had made it plain his interference into her personal life was unwelcome. If she wanted to dally with Randy, who was he to stop her?

Then he had kissed her. What had possessed him to kiss her like that this afternoon? He had been mad enough to strangle her, but he had sought another outlet for his emotions, one even more damaging. He wouldn't have been surprised if she had opened fire on him the minute he drove into the yard. Instead she was treating him like a king just returned to the castle.

"Hang your hat on the rack, Jake," she said. "And I don't think you'll need that gunbelt any more tonight."

"Banner, about this afternoon—"

"Never mind about that."

"Let me apologize."

"If you must, apologize to Randy. He hadn't done anything to warrant you pulling a gun on him."

"I intend to apologize to him tomorrow. I don't know what got into me." He spread his hands wide in a helpless gesture. "It's just that Ross told me to protect you, and when I heard you screaming—"

"I understand."

"And about the other—"

"Are you sorry you kissed me, Jake?"

Her face commanded all his attention. It shone pale and creamy in the golden lamplight, surrounded by the dark cloud of her hair. Her eyes were wide with inquiry, as though how he answered her question was of the utmost importance. Her lips were as tremulous and moist as if he had just kissed them.

His answer was no. But he couldn't admit it out loud, so he said nothing. He had behaved like a man possessed this afternoon when he saw Randy's hands on Banner. She was obviously jealous of Priscilla. Jealousy between them was dangerous. And he knew it. And the sooner he called an end to this cozy evening, the better. "I need to be getting—"

"No, wait." She took two rapid steps forward. When he looked at her as though she had taken leave of her senses, she fell back a step. Catching her hands at her waist, she said quickly, "I have a favor to ask. If you . . . if you have the time."

"What is it?"

"In the living room. I have a picture to hang and I wondered if you could help me with it."

He glanced over his shoulder toward the center room. One small lamp was burning in the corner. The room was cast in shadows, as intimate as those in the barn had been. The parlor was also the scene of the kiss that afternoon. Jake was better off not being reminded of that at all.

"I'm not much good at picture hanging," he hedged.

"Oh, well." She made a dismissive little wave with her hand. "You've put in a full day already and it isn't the foreman's job to hang pictures, I suppose."

Hell. Now she thought he didn't want to help her. She looked crestfallen, disappointed that she wouldn't get her picture hung and embarrassed for having asked his help and being turned down.

"I guess it wouldn't take too long, would it?"

"No, no," she said, lifting her head eagerly. "I have everything ready." She brushed past him on her way into the parlor. "I got the hammer and a nail from the barn this afternoon while you were gone. I tried to hang it myself, but couldn't tell if I was getting it in the right spot or not."

She was chattering breathlessly. Jake thought she might be as nervous as he about returning to this room. But she made no effort to turn up the lamp or light another one. Instead she made a beeline for the far wall.

Was this her way of telling him that she had forgiven his behavior that afternoon, that she wasn't afraid to be in an empty house with him long after the sun had gone down? Had everything she had done tonight been a peacemaking gesture? If so, he was grateful to her. They couldn't have gone on much longer without killing each other or . . .

The "or" he would do well not to think about. Especially since she was facing him again.

"I thought I'd hang it on this wall, about here," she said, pointing her finger and cocking her head to one side.

"That would be nice." He felt about as qualified to give advice on hanging a picture as he would be to choose a chapeau in a milliner's shop.

"About eye level?"

"Whose eye level? Yours or mine?"

She laughed. "I see what you mean." She scraped the top of her head with her palm and slid it horizontally until it bumped against his breastbone. "I only come to here on you, don't I?"

When she glanced up at him, his breath caught somewhere between his lungs and his throat. How could he have ever considered this creature with the bewitching eyes and teasing smile a child? He had been with whores who prided themselves on knowing all there was to know about getting a man's blood to the boiling point. But no woman had ever had an impact on him the way this one did. Except perhaps Lydia those months they were together on the wagon train.

His love for her had mellowed since then. He no longer experienced rushes of passionate desire every time he saw her. That summer traveling between Tennessee and Texas, he had been perpetually randy. Desire for Lydia, desire for Priscilla, desire for women, period.

He had been sixteen, the sap of youth flowing sweetly, but painfully, through his body. But that's what he felt like every time he looked at Banner. He felt sixteen again and with no more control over his body than he had then.

Her skirt was rustling against his pants. Her breasts were achingly close to his chest. She smelled too good for it to be legal. He could practically taste her breath as it softly struck his chin. Before he drowned in the swirling depths of her eyes, he said, "Maybe we'd better—"

"Oh, yes," she said briskly. Taking a three-legged stool from in front of an easy chair, she placed it near the wall and, raising her skirt above her ankles, stepped up on it. "The picture is there on the table. Hand it to me, please, then step back and tell me when it looks right."

He picked up the framed picture. "This is pretty."

It was a pastoral scene of horses grazing in a verdant pasture. "I thought it looked like Plum Creek." She glared at him, daring him to say anything derogatory about the name she had selected.

"I didn't say anything."

"No, but I know what you're thinking," she said accusingly. He only smiled benignly and passed her the picture.

She turned her back, raised her arms and positioned the picture. "How does that look?"

"A little lower maybe."

"There?"

"That's about right."

Keeping the picture flat against the wall, she craned her head around. "Are you really judging or are you just trying to get this over with?"

"I'm doing the best I can," he said, acting offended. "If you don't appreciate my help, you can always ask somebody else."

"Like Randy?"

Her taunt was intended as a joke, but Jake took it seriously. His brows gathered into a V above his nose as he took in the picture *she* made perched on that stool, leaning toward the wall with her arms raised. There was a good two inches of lacy petticoat showing above her trim ankles. Her rear end was sticking out. The apron's bow, topping that cute rounded bottom, was a tease no man could resist. The way her breasts poked out in front clearly defined their shape. No, not Randy. Not anybody if Jake could help it.

He considered the placement of the picture with more care this time. "A little to the left if you want it centered." She moved it accordingly. "There. That's perfect."

"All right. The nail will have to go in about six inches higher because of the cord it hangs by. Bring it and the hammer. You can drive it in while I hold the frame."

He did as he was told, straddling the stool and leaning around her. He tried to avoid touching her, adjusting his arms in several positions, none of them satisfactory.

"Just reach up between my arms with one hand and go over the top with the other."

He swallowed and held his breath, trying not to notice her breasts as his hand snaked up between them. He held the nail in place with the other, though that was no small task because he was shaking on the inside.

This was ridiculous! How many woman had he tumbled? Stop acting like a goddamn kid and just get the job done so you can get the hell out of here! he shouted inwardly.

Carefully he drew the hand holding the hammer back. But not carefully enough. His elbow pressed against her side. One of his knees bumped the back of hers. The backs of his knuckles sank into the plumpness of her breasts.

"Excuse me," he muttered.

"That's all right."

He struck the nail, praying it would go into the wall

with only one blow. It didn't. He moved his hand back and struck it again, and again, until he could see progress. Then, in rapid succession, he hit it viciously several times.

"That's good enough," he said gruffly, and withdrew his arms.

"Yes, I think so." Her voice sounded as unsteady as his.

She draped the silken cord around the head of the nail and leaned as far back as she could while still maintaining her balance on the stool.

"How's that?"

"Fine, fine." He laid the hammer on the nearest table and ran his sleeve over his perspiring forehead.

"Is it straight?"

"A little lower on the left."

"There?"

"Not quite."

"There?"

Damn, he cursed silently. He had to get out of here or he was going to explode. He strode forward, wanting to straighten the picture quickly so he could leave and get some much needed air to clear his head. But in his haste, the toe of his boot caught on one of the stool's three legs and it rocked perilously.

Banner squeaked in alarm and flailed her arms.

Life on the trail for so many years had given Jake reflexes as quick as summer lightning. His arms went around her faster than the blink of an eye and anchored her against him. When the stool clattered onto its side, Banner was being held several inches off the floor.

One of Jake's arms was around her waist, the other hand was flattened against her chest. Rather than letting her slide down, he lowered her. His back rounded slightly as he followed her down, bending over her.

But once her feet were safely on the floor, he didn't release her. Jake had spread his legs wide to break her fall. Now Banner's hips were tucked snugly in the notch between his thighs.

His cheek was lying along hers and when her nearness and her warmth and her scent got to be too much for him to resist, he turned his head and nuzzled her ear with his nose. His arms automatically tightened around her. He groaned her name.

How could anything that felt so right be so wrong? Lord, he wanted her. Knowing in his deepest self that what had happened that other time was an abomination against decency, he wanted her again. There was no use lying to himself that he didn't. He had hurt her once. He had sworn never to again. He had betrayed a friendship that meant more to him than anything in the world.

Yet such arguments were burned away like fog in a noonday sun as his lips moved in her hair and his nose breathed in the fragrance of the cologne that had been dabbed on that softest of spots behind her ear.

"Banner, tell me to leave you alone."

"I can't."

She moved her head to one side, giving him access. His lips touched her neck.

"Don't let this happen again."

"I want you to hold me."

"I want to, I want to."

He moved his hand from her chest up to her neck, then her chin, until his hand lightly covered her face. Through parted lips her breath was hot and quick on his palm.

Like a blind man, he charted each feature of her face with calloused fingertips suddenly sensitized to capture each nuance. He smoothed her brows, which he knew to be raven black and beautifully arched. His fingers coasted over her cheekbones. They were freckled. He had come to adore every single freckle. Her nose was perfect, if a bit impudent.

Her mouth.

His fingers brushed back and forth over her lips. They were incredibly soft. The warm breaths filtering through them left his fingers moist.

He pressed his mouth to her cheek, her ear, into her hair.

The hand at her waist opened wide over her midriff. He curled his fingers against the taut flesh. She whimpered. He argued with himself, but there was no stopping his hand from gliding up the corrugated perfection of her ribs and covering her breast. Their moans complemented each other.

Her ripe fullness filled his hand, and against his revolving thumb, the center of her breast tightened into a bead of arousal.

"Jake—"

"Sweet, so sweet."

"This happens sometimes."

"What?"

"That," she answered on a puff of air as his fingers closed around her nipple. "They get that way sometimes . . . when I look at you."

"Good God, Banner, don't tell me that."

"What does it mean?"

"It means I never should have stayed."

"And they won't go down. Not for the longest time. They stay like that, kind of itchy and tingling—"

"Oh, hush."

"—and that's when I wish—"

"What?"

"—that we were in the barn again and you were—"

"Don't say it."

"—inside me."

"Jesus, Banner, stop."

He made a cradle of his palm and laid it along her cheek, gradually turning her head to face him. And as her head turned, so did her body. The fabric of her clothes dragged against his like the tide on the seashore, separate, yet bound.

When their eyes met and locked hungrily, he lowered his mouth to hers. He thrust his tongue deep into her mouth as he pressed her hips against him.

He tore his mouth free. "No, Banner. I hurt you before, remember?"

"Yes, but that wasn't why I was crying."

"Then why?"

"Because it began to feel good and I . . . I thought you'd hate me for the way I was acting."

"No, no," he whispered fervently into her hair.

"You were so . . . big."

"I'm sorry."

"I just didn't expect it to be so . . . and . . . and so . . ."

"Did it feel good to you at all, Banner?"

"Yes, yes. But it was over too soon."

He laid his hard cheek against hers. His breathing was labored, otherwise he didn't move. "Too soon?"

"I felt like something was about to happen, but it didn't."

Jake was stunned. Could it be? He knew whores faked it. He didn't have any experience with decent women. Certainly not with virgins. Never with a virgin. He had never taken anyone he could feel tenderness for.

But tenderness for Banner enveloped him now. He cupped her face between his hands and went searching in her eyes for the truth. He saw no fear there, only a keen desire that matched his own. Making a growling sound deep in his throat, he lowered his head again.

"Hello!" a cheerful voice called out. "Anyone at home?"

Only then did they become aware of the jingle of harnesses and the unmistakable sounds of a wagon being pulled to a halt outside.

"Banner? Where are you?"

It was Lydia.

LOVESWEPT

*Love Stories you'll never forget
by authors you'll always remember*

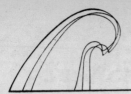

LOVESWEPT

Love Stories you'll never forget by authors you'll always remember

 # LOVESWEPT

Love Stories you'll never forget by authors you'll always remember

Prices and availability subject to change without notice.

Buy them at your local bookstore or use this handy coupon for ordering:

LOVESWEPT

Love Stories you'll never forget by authors you'll always remember